Phyllis Reynolds Naylor

FOOTPRINTS AT THE WINDOW

The York Trilogy
BOOK THREE

SCHOLASTIC INC.
New York Toronto London Auckland Sydney

The map of the advance of the Black Death
is adapted from *Black Death* by Philip Ziegler.
New York: Harper, 1971.

ISBN 0-590-46511-2

12 11 10 9 8 7 6 5 4 3 2 1   2 3 4 5 6 7/9

Printed in the U.S.A.   40

First Scholastic printing, September 1992

For the heirs to the eighties,
with hope

PROLOGUE

SOME TIME about 1000 A.D., somewhere in India, the first band of gypsies began a westward movement across the continent.

No one is sure why they left or from where it was, exactly, that they started, but today their Romany language is similar in many respects to the languages of the lands through which they passed. Some believe that there is a kinship between the gypsies and the ancient Celtic Druids; Irishmen have been known to say that if they hum a few measures of an old Irish ballad, a man from India can usually finish the melody instinctively. What is fact, however, is that after wandering across Asia and then Europe, some Romanies reached the British Isles in the early 1500s.

There were other travelers in the middle ages, however, who were neither Indian, Irish, nor Celt. These were the early traders, who journeyed in caravans from Europe to Asia, bringing back treasures of the Orient. But in the year 1346, along with silks and teas and spices, something terrible accompanied the merchants home, and it was called the Black Death.

It was passed on to a warrior horde that was besieging a Genoese trading post in the Crimea. Their leader, seeing that their own death was certain, ordered that the plague-infested corpses should be catapulted into the town.

Disease immediately broke out, and twelve Genoese galleys, fleeing the sickness, entered the harbor of Messina in 1347. From there, the plague covered all of Sicily. Ships from Messina, in turn, carried the disease to Italy, and then the entire continent lay helpless before the ravages of a terrifying epidemic.

In August of 1348, a shipload of desperate survivors put out from Calais, France, hoping to find refuge in the still plague-free island of Britain. Their ship docked in Dorset and by the end of the year, all of southwest England was stricken. Having begun at the seacoast, the plague worked its way through the interior. In 1349, it reached the town of York.

The Black Death did not come to America, still undiscovered. And whatever illnesses the later immigrants brought, they did not, fortunately, bring the plague. But the westward trek of the gypsies continued and—like the flow of ocean currents—they crossed the Atlantic in the late 1700s. Many chose the banks of the Susquehanna River as their home.

It is both here and there and then and now that the story is concluded.

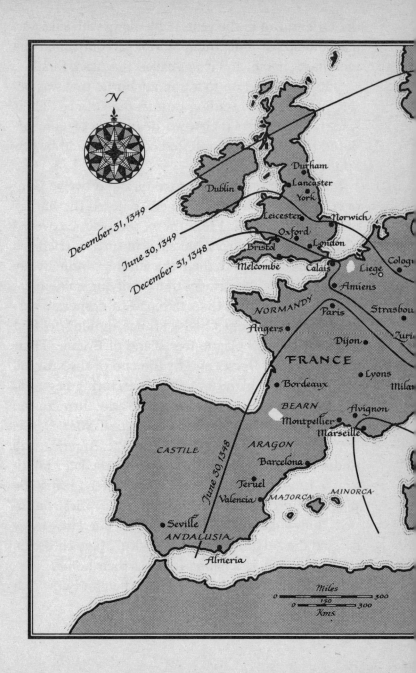

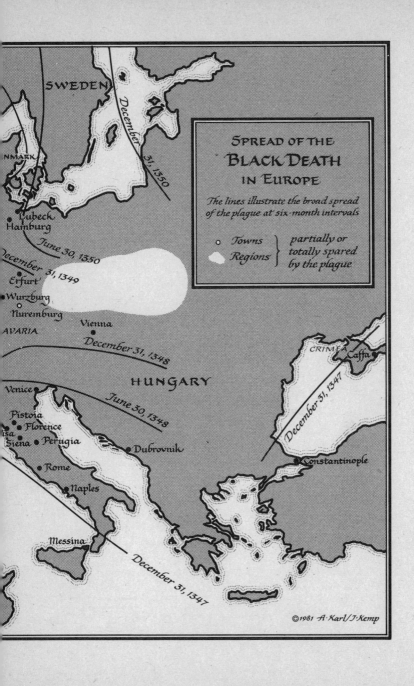

SWEDEN

December 31, 1350

NMARK

Lubeck
Hamburg

June 30, 1350

December 31, 1349

Erfurt
Wurzburg
Nuremburg

AVARIA

Vienna

December 31, 1348

HUNGARY

June 30, 1348

Venice
Pistoia
Florence
isa Siena Perugia
Dubrovnik
Rome
Naples

Messina

December 31, 1347

CRIMEA Caffa

December 31, 1347

Constantinople

SPREAD OF THE BLACK DEATH IN EUROPE

The lines illustrate the broad spread
of the plague at six-month intervals

○ Towns } partially or
Regions } totally spared
by the plague

©1981 A·Karl/J·Kemp

FOOTPRINTS
AT THE
WINDOW

1

"When has any such thing ever been heard of or seen? In what histories has it been read that houses were left vacant, cities deserted, the country neglected, and a fearful and universal solitude over the whole earth? Will Posterity ever believe these things when we, who have seen them, can hardly credit them?"

—Petrarch [1304–1374]

HE NO LONGER heard his name, he heard footsteps. They came when he least expected them, and Dan could not tell if they were above or below or beside him. But they were there, like a heartbeat—now fainter, now more distinct—

3

and then they would disappear altogether, only to come again when his mind was on other things.

"There're gypsies about," Blossom said that morning over her white tea—white, she called it, because she took it with cream. "I've seen their smoke over the woods—just a wisp, but it's there."

Dan watched her from across the table. Like the flat stump of an old tree, her face seemed to have a line for every year of her life. "How can you tell they're gypsies?" he asked.

"I know the signs." Blossom clicked her teeth. "There was a rooster missing yesterday—the red bantam with the lame leg. They do that, you know. If they take something from you, they'll not pick the finest, but something with a defect, just to salve their conscience. They're not stealing, mind you, just thinning things out a bit." The laugh lines at the corners of her eyes deepened.

"Have you seen anyone about?"

"Not yet."

He stood on the back porch and looked out over the south pasture. Just as Blossom had said, smoke rose up over the woods beyond and hovered there against the blue of the sky, a thin curl, like a question mark.

He would not go searching them out—not yet, anyway. As long as he had the coin, the ancient Roman denarius, secure in the slit of his watchband, the gypsies would come to him, he was sure of it. Ever since Nat had traded it to him in York last spring for his belt, the Faws had been wild to get it back. He would wait.

Lonnie, the young man whom Bee had hired for the summer, was gone. There was work from the time Dan got up in the morning until he fell exhausted into bed at night—clipping shrubs, chopping wood, digging, hoeing—mindless chores that taxed his strength but not his head. Lonnie had left early the day of the storm and not come back. It did not bother Blossom particularly. She had raised children of her own, and she knew when a young man was getting restless, she said, eager to be off and about, by now he was far up the river. But Dan stood at the door, watching the smoke, and wasn't so sure.

"They've been through here before, the gypsies?" he asked later as he hoed with his grandmother in the garden.

Blossom bent down and rummaged through the green of the cucumber leaves. Her face glowed in the heat of the sun, and even her scalp was pink beneath the sparse strands of white hair.

"Every now and then," she replied, and straightened up slowly, one hand to her back. "Used to be I'd see them right often—when I was a young bride—every summer or two. The children would knock on my door selling violets and snowdrops or watercress. But now there are long stretches—years, even—when I don't see them at all, and just when I've decided they're gone for good, there's their smoke once more." She squinted toward the woods in the distance. "I don't mind them taking my rooster; it's comforting to an old soul like me to have them return, like one of earth's cycles, you know. There're times I've suspected that on a particularly wet night, they've come up across the south pasture and spent the night in my barn, but I don't care a bit. Only once did I take them to task."

Carrying the cucumbers in her apron, Blossom shuffled over to the bench under the beech tree and sat down, smiling to herself. "I'd left my wash on the line overnight, and first thing I saw the next morning were two gypsy women looking my dresses over. One woman was in red—a long skirt down to the ankles —and the other in blue, and they were fingering my good yellow dress with the purple flowers, feeling it, you know, to test the cloth. I stuck my head out the window and called, 'Not my yellow dress, ladies. Help yourself to the green one down there on the end if you like, but the yellow one I'm wearing to Harrisburg next Sunday.' "

She chuckled. "And you know, they bowed— curtsied, sort of, the way they do in England to the Queen—and took the green dress with a 'Thank you, mum.' The next morning I found me a bouquet of flowers on my doorstep, and by the time I got them in and on the table, I realized they were my own geraniums." Both she and Dan laughed out loud. Blossom wiped her eyes in merriment. "That's why I like to see the smoke above the trees. Like old friends, that's what the gypsies are, here to pay me a visit."

When would they come, then—that night? Dan

wondered, listening to a light rain fall as he and Blossom ate their supper. Would the gypsies be content this time to sleep in the barn or pick the flowers or go off with another chicken? Or would they come inside and up to his room, looking for the Roman denarius?

It wasn't till later, when he and his grandmother sat in the parlor, the windows open and the breeze blowing through, that they heard the horse whinny.

Blossom put down the mystery story she was reading and leaned forward, her head cocked slightly, her good ear toward the barn. "Lord, now, they wouldn't be taking my horse, would they?"

"I'll have a look around," Dan said, and got up.

He took the kerosene lamp from the nail by the cellar door and went out the back. Pausing on the doorstep, he watched for shadows, for movement, for the glow of a cigarette, perhaps. He saw nothing.

He walked across the clearing to the barn and unlatched the heavy door, then shone the light inside. The cow watched as he moved slowly toward the other end, between the stalls and the bales of hay stacked on one side. When he reached the horse, however, it was standing with head down, asleep. Nothing was amiss. Nothing out of place. He wondered.

Latching the barn door behind him again, he turned toward the house where a patch of light from the parlor window fell onto the bare ground. He moved around the house checking the woodpile, the shrubs, the shed. When he reached the square of light again, however, he saw them—large footprints there in the damp earth. They came, it seemed, from out of the darkness and stopped, facing the open window. Then they turned and went on, disappearing once more into the shadows.

Early the next morning, when Dan looked out his bedroom window, he saw a gray horse grazing in the south pasture. But by the time he had put on his boots and jeans and gone out himself to the meadow, the horse was gone.

THERE WAS A LETTER that afternoon from Joe Stanton, the cab driver whom Dan had met in York:

Dear Dan:
I received your letter and, knowing how eager Ambrose was to have word of you, went looking for the Faws last Sunday. They were half the way to Pickering, but I was able to catch them before they moved on.
Ambrose is much distressed at your request. Of course you are right in asking for the return of your belt in exchange for the Roman denarius, but the truth of the matter is that the belt is gone. It seems that after discovering you had left York with the coin, Ambrose rode his horse down into the Ouse in a fit of anger and flung your belt into the river. It's a way with gypsies, you see.

He had not thought at the time that there was any chance of contacting you again, and only later did he think of me. I can only tell you, for Ambrose's sake, how desperately he wants the silver denarius in the family's possession again and will double his offer of money if you will only post it at once.

There is another matter of which I write, and I trust that my letters to you are private, for I am certain that no one but ourselves would understand. The ghostly soldiers have returned to me since your visit here. I did not seek them out. In fact, I have been most reluctant to think of them since we wrestled that night on the moor. But they have come to me, and not only have I marched with them, compelled by some force which I do not understand, but I was their centurion.

It was not clear to me as to where we were exactly or what we were about. All I know is that I and my men were surrounded by a strange sort of people, and I was desperate for a means of escape. I seemed to be looking for someone to slip through enemy lines and go for help. What will happen next, I can only wonder. It seems I am destined to play out a scene that happened once near York when the Romans were here. I feel that the story is not yet over, that there is a battle yet to be. I worry that perhaps you are caught up in this also.

I beg you to reconsider about the coin. There can be no question that it means much more to Ambrose than it does to you. On the other hand, I have a strange premonition that I should not be asking you—that for my own sake, perhaps, it would be better if you kept the denarius. This makes no sense at all, but I have long given up trying to see the logic of these episodes.

Orlenda asked about you. She stopped me just as I was leaving, as though she didn't want her father to hear. She wanted to know if you were all right, and I told her that, to the best of my knowledge, you were in good health.

With kind regards,
Joe

DAN SAT ON HIS BED and stared at the letter's post-mark. It had been mailed two weeks before. Somehow, since that time, he had been back to York. He had been there with Orlenda around the year 400 A.D.—near the end of the Roman occupation—and had helped her break away from her home on the moor. He had left her and her sister in Eboracum and promised to go on to a place called Deva with her brother Nat to see if the land beyond was indeed a land of peace as her mother had remembered.

Since writing this letter, then, Joe must have encountered the ghosts a second time; it was then he had wrestled Dan to the ground and given him a silver denarius, commanding him to go at once to Eboracum for reinforcements. The future battle that Joe had referred to had already been, and there were no victors. Nat had deserted, and Rose, his mother, had walked into the midst of the fighting with a torch held high, sending the Romans reeling in astonishment while the tribesmen held back out of respect.

Both Ambrose Faw, the "last of the Brigantes," as he had called himself, and Joe Stanton, the centurion, had survived, as their fortunes had predicted, for whatever happened to one must also happen to the other. Two powerful men, and they would either destroy themselves or they would make their peace. For now, at least, they lived, and the story continued, and the animosity went on.

Twice then, Dan had been given a Roman denarius, yet there was in his watchband only one. Was it Nat's or the centurion's? And what should he do now? For the last few days, having called out Ambrose's name in the cellar, Dan had returned to the spring again and again, waiting for a face to appear in the water as it had done before. He had stooped over the spring and stared down into the crevice in the rock from which it sprang, daring the ghosts to come forward. But there were no faces, no voices, no shadows.

Wait, his senses told him. He thought of Orlenda, of the possibility that she might need him. It was this possibility that gave his life meaning. His own future was a question mark, a wildly unpredictable gamble, but there was something he could do for her, and he wanted that chance.

He waited, and in the days to come, nothing else seemed to matter. To see her again, to become a part of her life and know that he would be remembered —this was a thought that absorbed him completely. August was half over, but he didn't care. He gave no thought to school or the newspaper staff or the article he had promised to write, for the future somehow lay behind him, decided upon already, and it was the past that lay ahead. Crazy.

He moved about the place in slow motion, repeating tasks he had already done and neglecting others. He would spend an hour leaning on the fence at the end of the south pasture, facing the woods beyond, or lie on the back porch glider, one foot on the floor, rocking gently, his mind beyond the roof, the trees, the sky, even. At dinner he would find himself staring at the same piece of potato he thought he had eaten but that he had not, in fact, even raised to his mouth.

"You know what I think?" his grandmother said at last. "You're coming down with something, that's what." Her faded blue eyes, like small islands in a sea of wrinkles, watched him from across the table. "The day that Lonnie left, when you were mucking about in the rain. . . . Lord, Dan! You should have had better sense! Drenched to the skin, that's what you were. You've been incubating something ever since."

It was as good an excuse as any.

"Maybe so," he said.

Blossom stirred her tea as she studied him. "Viruses will do that, you know—creep inside you and wait. Then all of a sudden you're sick and can't tell what it was that got to you."

There were a lot of things lying in wait for him these days—ghosts of the past, robbers of his future. . . .

"You're right, Bee," he said finally, getting up. "I'm probably catching something. Guess I'll go to bed early and try to sleep it off."

But he did not sleep so easily. Rest came fitfully —bits of semi-consciousness alternating with dreams. And the dreams were much the same, that someone, somewhere, was waiting for him—a soldier, a gypsy, a girl. Whatever was expected of him in the dreams, he never seemed able to do; wherever he tried to go, obstacles rose up in his path. He was pulled this way and that, and accomplished one thing only at the expense of another. He awoke bathed in perspiration, his heart pounding, and threw off his sheet, waiting for the agitation to subside.

He sat up at last and turned on the light, letting the familiar sights of the room calm him. Leaning back against the brass bedstead, he studied the copper lamp on the ceiling, the patterned wallpaper, the patchwork quilt on the chest, and the picture on the opposite wall of a storm at sea.

He propped his pillow behind his head and looked at it. For sixteen years—ever since he could remember, at least—he had been looking at that picture of a sinking ship. The billowy seas, the white foam, the men in the water, and the captain there on the prow deciding what to do: jump overboard and chance it or go down with the ship. Dan guessed, from the look of quiet resignation on the man's face, that he would go down. Why was it that heroes never looked terrified? Why did they always look so accepting—bored, even?

He got up and wandered about the room, staring for a long time out the south window into the darkness and seeing nothing. Then he ambled over to the bureau, studying the old family portraits there on top.

There was a picture of him and his parents when he was five—Dan seated on a new tricycle, a smile as wide as a cantaloupe on his face. There were great-uncles and second cousins he never knew, and a photo of his father and Aunt Shirley when they were teenagers, sitting sedately, carefully groomed, on the front steps. So that's the way Dad looked when he was Dan's age. He turned the photo over to see if there was a date on the back. In Blossom's hand was the notation, "Brian, 17, Shirley, 14½."

All of the photos, he discovered, were labeled on the back, and he tried to separate those who had Huntington's disease from those who did not. There was no way of knowing, of course. He had forgotten the names on the family tree that his mother had so carefully researched and circled. So he made a game of trying to determine which of the faces looked neurologically disoriented, which of the expressions were preludes to brain deterioration and madness. He studied each face, then turned the photo over to check the name on the back. They all sounded very old and far away.

At one side of the bureau was a small framed tintype, obviously the oldest of them all. It was the picture of a woman, done in shades of brown, and she was dressed in a high-collared blouse, her hair like a puffy flat pillow around her head. Dan turned it over to see the name, and there, in handwriting so faint he could barely make it out, were the words, "Suzanna Faa."

Slowly he turned the picture over, studying the face, then turned it again and stared at the name. Faa. Was there a connection somehow? Was it more than a coincidence?

He had just started back toward his bed when he heard them again—the footsteps.

THEY WERE SO CLEAR, so distinct, that he was certain now they were in the attic. Always before when he had gone off to check—the cellar, the porch, the hallway—he had found nothing. It was like chasing phantoms. They were either before or behind or above or below, always at a point he could not reach. But this time they were so obviously overhead that he could almost point to the place on the ceiling from where they came.

He quickly pulled on his jeans and got the flashlight from his dresser. With ears straining for the slightest sound, he moved out into the hall and made his way to the ladder at the end. Quietly, cautiously, he began the climb. With each step he stopped, waiting, listening, then took another. The footsteps went on—heavy, ponderous things, like those of a distraught man, pacing.

He reached the top and put the flat of his hand on the center of the door, pushing gently. It did not budge.

Again he tried to push open the door, shoving against it with both hands, holding the flashlight between his knees. One edge raised slightly, but the lid had jammed with dust and disuse.

Afraid that if he did not hurry, the night walker might elude him, Dan moved up another step and, putting his back to the door, raised up quickly with all his strength. The door flew open and tumbled, with a bang, onto the attic floor.

Instantly the air was filled with the screech of birds, the flapping of wings, the rustle of feathers. Stepping up higher, with his body halfway through the opening, Dan quickly shone the light around and saw an entire flock of magpies circling low, sweeping their wingtips against the sloping roof. Then, as though flying in formation, they all headed to the window in the west wall and flew out. Just as the last was disappearing, Dan saw a shadow go with them, as large as a man, as gray as smoke, moving through the window like mist, then mingling with the night.

A wild shaking came over him, and Dan clutched himself tightly, his teeth chattering. A chill wind followed in the wake of the birds, a clammy dampness.

He replaced the trapdoor and was halfway down the ladder when he saw Blossom standing in the hallway below, her robe about her, hair long and loose, like a priestess from another age. She was holding the kerosene lamp high in her hand, and huge shadows bobbed about on the walls. The cat stood beside her, its tail switching.

"What is it, Dan?"

He tried to stop the shaking, to control his voice. "Birds. They must have nests up there."

"That's all, then? I heard an awful banging."

"I knocked the door open to see what all the commotion was. They flew out through the window."

"What were they? Starlings?"

Dan hesitated. "Magpies, Bee."

"*Magpies?* Where on earth do you suppose they're from?"

"I don't know."

She studied him a minute, then slowly lowered the lamp. "Well, best we screen it up, I suppose."

"Yeah, I guess so."

Bee turned and started back down the stairs. "I'm going to fix something hot to drink, Dan. Come have a cup with me."

"No, but I'll sit with you while you drink it. I'm not very sleepy."

He followed her to the kitchen and watched as she shuffled from refrigerator to stove, pouring milk into a pan and finally into her cup. Her long white hair covered her shoulders like a cape, wavy from the braid that she wore twisted on top of her head.

"No good going to bed early if you're going to wake up in the night," she said, sitting down across from him.

"Don't worry." He fingered the fringed cloth on the table, choosing his words carefully: "I was looking at the old photos up on the bureau in my room, Bee. Quite a collection—people I never heard of."

"My rogue's gallery." Blossom chuckled. "No use

folks having their pictures taken if they're going to be shut away in a box. When the top of the piano got full and then the mantel, the pictures sort of found their way upstairs. They do get a bit dusty, but at least they're out in the fresh air."

"What was your maiden name? I've forgotten."

"Myles, spelled with a 'y.' "

"Oh." Dan thought for a moment. "There's an old photo up there I'm curious about. On the back it says 'Suzanna Faa.' "

Blossom sipped at her milk. "That was my grandmother, on my mother's side. Pretty thing, wasn't she? Well, I suppose not to you, because everybody looked as though they had indigestion when they posed back then. But she did have a lovely smile, and the nicest teeth. The tinker's daughter, that's who she was."

Dan sat riveted to his chair, unmoving—his lungs like stone, almost unable to breathe. The tinker—the man whose face appeared in the cellar spring, who Blossom swore was her great grandfather. Dan knew who he really was, however—the gypsy, Ambrose Faw, who had somehow followed him here. Was this the connection? Was this what made him part of the ghostly happenings in England, what took him back to the town of York centuries before his time?

Perhaps his blood was partly that of the dark-eyed gypsies from India whom he had studied about in school—the gypsies who made their way through Turkey and France and on across the channel—who mingled their blood in turn with the descendants of the Celts, of Roman legionaries, and of the fierce warriors of Caledonia. He was a citizen of the world first, of that he was sure. He loved his country, but his allegiance was to all of humanity, from which he had sprung.

"It's a strange spelling," he said at last.

"That it is. Suzanna, she was the only one of the children who kept to her father's spelling of it. The others took an 'a' off the end and put a 'w' in its place. My great-grandfather, they said, used to brag that *his* great-grandfather had made such a nuisance of himself in Scotland that he was banished along with eight other gypsies and transported to Virginia, one of the first Romanies ever to set foot in America." She chuckled. "Now some people, I suppose, would keep a thing like that to themselves, but my great-grandfather, he thrived on it." She wiped her mouth on the sleeve of her robe when she thought that Dan wasn't looking. "I think I would have liked that man. The stories, they say, he could tell. . . ."

She put down her cup, her blue eyes suddenly serious. "I talk to him sometimes, you know," she confessed. "It sounds like I'm balmy, I suppose, but ever since that day I saw his face in the stream, I've figured he came for a purpose, not just for his health. So I sit me here in the kitchen some nights and leave the cellar door ajar, and I listen. I tell him there's a chair across from me, should he care to pay me a visit. It wouldn't scare me, you know—not a bit. But he never comes—not yet, anyway."

There was uncommon courage in the little

woman across the table, Dan decided, studying her face. Whether she viewed the ghostly apparition as the old tinker himself or as a messenger of death, come to carry her off, there was no running away on her part. She faced it head on.

"Once you started talking, Bee," he joked, "he wouldn't get a word in edgewise. The old tinker knows he's better off down there in the cellar. You want somebody to talk to, I'll go round up the neighbors."

They laughed then, and Blossom went off to bed with the smell of milk on her breath, her eyes heavy once more with sleep.

Upstairs, standing at the window, Dan felt as though he had been injected with his grandmother's courage. He thought again of Orlenda, determined to go to her, to see her one last time. The coin, he felt sure, was the way. If the gypsies did not come in a few more days, he would seek them out.

2

ORNINGS MINGLED with afternoons, and afternoons with evenings. The period from dusk to dawn was a profusion of fears and murmurings and unsettling dreams, punctuated by a cold sweat.

The hours passed in slow motion, and the cow and horse sought the shade, stunned by the heat. An occasional breeze startled them, as though something foreign were in the air, as though dry earth and parched grass and a broiling noonday sun were the way things were meant to be.

Dan went about his tasks mechanically. He was tanned and the muscles in his arms were stronger, but his body itself was lean—thinner than when he had arrived. At the supper table Blossom would watch him anxiously, pushing the platter of chicken or corn toward him an inch at a time, as if perhaps he had overlooked it. But he ate only a few bites and felt full.

Each evening, before darkness settled in, he would stand on the back porch and look out over the south pasture; and again, if the smoke was there, it rose like a ghostly apparition above the trees. The wait went on.

Friday morning, however, there was a visitor. Dan had just gone up to the attic to measure the window for a piece of screen. He heard a car pull in the drive and, looking out, saw Bill—editor of his school paper—opening the door of his old Buick.

By the time Dan got downstairs, Blossom had Bill in the parlor with a glass of iced tea in his hand and had already extracted a promise that he would stay for lunch.

"Bill! For crying out loud! What are you doing down here?" Dan grabbed him by the shoulder and sat down across from him.

Bill grinned. "Had the day off and thought I'd come down and see what you were up to. I don't have to be at the car wash till four, and your grandmother's already said she'd feed me."

Dan smiled. "All you have to do around here is slow down on the road out front and Bee has an extra plate on the table. Isn't that right, Bee?"

Blossom smiled. "Maybe with someone else to look at besides me, the lad will eat a decent meal," she said to Bill confidentially. "Skin and bones. That's what he is."

"So how you doing?" Bill asked him.

"Oh, not bad. Surviving the heat. That's about all."

"What you ought to do," put in Blossom, "is go down in the woods for a swim. That'll cool you off quick."

Dan did not want to go. He wanted to seek out the gypsies in his own time, in his own way, and he certainly did not want Bill around when he did. But it was too late.

"Man, that sounds great to me," said Bill. "Harrisburg is like an oven—heat waves over the sidewalk so thick they make you dizzy."

Dan hesitated. The place where the water was deepest was just beyond the fence and the walnut grove, some distance from where he had seen the smoke. He'd chance it, but he didn't want to have to explain anything more to Bill.

"You like your chicken hot or cold?" Blossom called after them as they set out across the pasture. "I've got some leftover pieces I can warm up."

"I like everything cold in this weather," Bill called back. "Don't go to any bother. A chicken leg and a glass of milk will do fine."

The easy banter stopped as suddenly as the screen door closed again behind Blossom. For a few minutes the two tramped on through the grass, taller now since Lonnie was no longer there to do the mowing. Bill glanced over at Dan from time to time, but said nothing. Then finally the words came out: "Dan, you look awful. You know it?"

Dan kept his eyes on the trees ahead. "What do you mean?"

"Cheeks sunken in, your collar bone sticks out—

what in heck's wrong? I knew something was up when I didn't get your story like you'd promised. You haven't even started it, have you?"

Dan hadn't even thought about it. *A Gypsy Burial* —that was the story he had said he'd write for the first issue of the school paper—a lead-off article on student travel. Bill had set aside a whole page for it, and Dan was to recount the death of the old gypsy grandmother out on the moor beyond York. But he could not seem to focus his mind on writing, on words. There were other things he had to do.

"No," he said finally. "I haven't even started it."

Bill exhaled loudly, whistling slightly through his teeth, and they tramped on. They came to the fence at the end of the pasture and started through the walnut grove, then went on to the place where Blossom's stream met Little Donegal Creek, making a small pool, five feet deep, shady and dark.

They stood on the bank and stripped off their clothes, and it was only when Dan saw Bill's stocky body, the thigh muscles bulging, the thick shoulders, that he realized how anemic he must look in comparison. But his arms, at least, were strong, and he dived in, letting his body sink slowly, luxuriously, to the bottom. He surfaced and swam from one end to the other with only two strokes.

Shock therapy, that's what it was. He felt better, and a moment later he and Bill were both laughing, horsing about, hitting the water with upturned palms, sending spray into each other's faces. The water blurred their eyes and matted their lashes. They ducked each other and rolled over and over like otters, chasing around and around the pond—evading, diving, surfacing once again until at last, thoroughly cooled and exhausted, they swam over to the edge and sat down, waist deep in the water.

"Hey, man, this is living," Bill panted. "If I worked this farm, I'd spend half my time down here." He closed his eyes and tilted his face toward the trees above, letting a few flickers of sunlight play on his brow, glint against the red hair. Then he opened his eyes again and looked over at Dan. "Well, what is it? What's going on with you?"

Dan did not return his glance, and his lips barely moved when he answered. "What are you talking about?"

"Oh, cut it out, Dan. Quit playing games. Something's got you down and I think it's probably your dad. I heard he was in the hospital a couple weeks ago and figured you must be worried about him. And then, when your story never came, I decided to drive down and check."

If he admitted to only half his problems, Dan wondered, would that be good enough?

"Yeah, I am pretty worried, I guess. I don't think about it all the time, though. It's more like—well, a rock in the pit of the stomach. You know what I mean? Whenever I think I'm happy, when I feel really good, I remember, and then it's like something blew out the candle, snuffed out the joy."

Bill watched him, waiting, raising up in the water so that he could rest his arms on the bank behind. "What's the matter with him?"

"Huntington's disease. Maybe."

"What's that?"

Dan sighed inaudibly. He had to dredge it up with effort. There were other worries more pressing right now, things far too eerie to explain. He didn't need this one on his back again. But Bill had asked.

"It's something hereditary. Dad either has the defective gene or he doesn't. If he does, it works eventually on the brain cells—a slow deterioration, physically and mentally. A great way to go, huh?" He had not meant for the sarcasm to slip in, but it came anyway.

"When did you find out he had it?"

"We didn't. I mean, we're not sure yet. He's been having symptoms, that's all, and the hospital was checking them out. They didn't come up with anything definite."

"If he does have it, is there anything they can do?"

"No. Or for me either."

Bill looked at him sharply. "You'd get it, too?"

"If Dad has it, I have a fifty-fifty chance."

There was silence for a moment. Then, "Can't you get tested or anything? I mean, when will you know?"

"Not until I'm forty or older."

"Oh, Jeez!" Bill leaned back on the bank again,

his back arched tensely, arms spread out on the grass beside him, staring up at the trees, unblinking. "It's . . . it's almost worse, isn't it—not knowing—like you're always waiting for the other shoe to drop."

"That's how I feel exactly. It's how I've felt ever since last spring in York, when my parents finally told me."

Bill looked over at him again. "You've known since then? You didn't tell me."

Dan shrugged and said nothing.

"We've known something was wrong, though," Bill went on. "Judith Mott said something to me just before school was out—about how withdrawn you seemed. In fact, she called me last week and wondered if I'd heard from you—wondered where you were. She's copyeditor this year, you know. I guess it was partly her phone call and partly my own concern that made me drive down here."

"I don't need anybody to watch over me."

Bill studied him quietly. "I didn't say watch over you. But you need someone to talk to. You've got to spill your guts once in a while—really cut loose. You can't keep it all in. Judith really likes you; you can't help but know that."

Dan gave him a quick glance and felt his forehead knotting into a frown that he didn't really want to be there. "Well, she'd better get interested in someone else. Listen, Bill, I can't plan for anything. My future is one big question mark."

"That doesn't mean you can't have friends. If

everyone wanted a guarantee before they let anybody get close to them, we'd all be living in solitary confinement."

The frown seemed to disintegrate on its own, and Dan was glad to let it go. He needed Bill here, he knew, and was glad he had come. "Yeah, I guess so," he said finally.

"You know," Bill continued, "in a way, it's sort of like waiting for the 'Bomb,' isn't it? It's there, but nobody really knows if it will ever go off. The odds, the experts say, as the bombs keep piling up, are that at least some of them will. But nobody knows for sure. So we wait."

He slid down in the water until only his head was resting on the bank behind him. "The difference, I guess, is that if you get Huntington's disease, you go it alone—you and the other people who have it, I mean. But if somebody presses the button, we all go together. I can't know exactly what you're feeling, Dan, but I know some of it. I think about war all the time, see. I'm obsessed with it, and sometimes I'm so full of it I almost want to puke. I look at other people and wonder if they ever worry, too."

"Then I'm not the only one who keeps things in," Dan said. "Sounds like you need to cut loose once in a while, too—let everything hang out."

"Yeah, you're right. Nobody likes to go around being a crepe hanger, though. Everyone else seems to go about laughing and joking, like the world's going to go on forever, so I do too. And sometimes I really feel good—happy, optimistic. And then, other times, I wonder if down underneath everybody's as scared as I am—if they just don't show it."

He sat up again and leaned forward, resting his arms on his knees. "The awful, horrible thing is that war doesn't have to be. It's not like an earthquake or a bolt of lightning or something—a calamity we can't help. But to think that we might do ourselves in— that somebody just might be stupid enough or panicky enough or angry enough to press the button. ..." He filled his lungs with air and then slowly let it out, his shoulders sinking. "If I were you, Dan, I think I would be furious against the government, the generals, anybody who helps spend billions of dollars for bombs and weapons when the money could go for research on disease. That would just tear me up."

"Sometimes I think of that too."

"Jeez, it's like living in a lunatic asylum, isn't it?"

"But what's the solution?"

"To war, you mean?" Bill slowly shook his head. "That's the sticky part, isn't it? There are intelligent people saying different things. My uncle says we need more troops, more guns, more missiles to keep ourselves strong and keep the peace; Dad says that only keeps the arms race going, makes both sides more tense, and brings the day closer when one side or the other will strike first. They really go at it sometimes. Who's right?"

"I don't know. But uncertainty is hard to take, and I can see somebody wanting to jump the gun, to

meet it head on, just to get it over with. I know that from my own problem. And yet . . . there are times I've wondered if there really *was* a test to see if I was going to get Huntington's disease, would I really want to take it? Would I really want to know? Maybe there's something that holds us back in spite of ourselves." Dan jerked his head suddenly, for he thought he saw something moving off in the trees.

"What is it?" Bill asked.

"It . . . it looked like a gray horse," Dan said. "Do you see anything?"

"No. . . ."

Dan got up out of the water and pulled on his jeans.

"Come on," he said. "We'd better get back. Bee's probably got lunch waiting."

THEY CONTINUED their conversation after lunch—after Blossom had cajoled Bill into eating a mound of potato salad and tried to persuade him to stay overnight as well. When at last she had gone off to the north bedroom for her afternoon nap, Dan and Bill went out to the glider on the back porch, catching the occasional breeze that passed through the screening. They sat at opposite ends, rocking gently, the cat curled up between them.

"How does a person ever get used to it, Bill—to something hanging over him all the time? That's what I want to know. I think of college ahead of me and wonder why I even bother when something could happen before I graduate; if not to me, then to my father, but that would bring it all the closer."

Bill's foot stopped pushing on the floor for a moment, the rocking slowed, and then suddenly it began again.

"Listen," he said. "I've got a better one for you. Ever hear of a supernova?"

"I think so."

"It's a huge cosmic explosion, see, that could vaporize the earth, and some mathematical astronomer says we're five hundred million years overdue."

"That's supposed to make me feel better?"

"No, it's supposed to make you feel numb—to realize that we can spend all our time worrying about one thing when all the while something else is sneaking up behind us. Oh, heck. . . ."

He stopped rocking and stretched out his legs in front of him, his eyes on the pasture beyond the barn. "I lie in bed and think what the world would be like if there really was a nuclear war. Generals talk about it as though it's a possibility, like it's something they could win, Civil Defense calls certain buildings shelter areas, and the whole thing sounds like a bunch of kids playing war on the kitchen table."

"Yeah, I saw a map once of what just one bomb —a small one—could do to Philadelphia," Dan said. "The blast zone, the fire-storm zone, the lethal radiation zone. . . ."

"And even if you survive, nobody seems to talk about how the soil and the rivers and the air will be radioactive, what your odds would be of dying of leukemia. If Philadelphia goes, and New York and Boston, where do we get our medicines? How many doctors and hospitals will be left? Politicians talk as though we're playing a game of chicken with Russia —that whoever blinks first loses. We all lose, and nobody seems to realize it."

He sat without moving, as though paralyzed by the thought of it. "Anyway, I think about this and just go cold all over. I wonder how anybody can get up in the morning and go to school or work when the human race might be on the verge of making itself extinct. And then I remember the supernova and I think, wouldn't it be ironical if the stars beat us to it —if just when some lamebrain was about to push the button, the supernova would vaporize us all?"

Dan studied him, seeing a side of Bill he had never suspected was there before.

"I don't know. One way or another, it's all over, isn't it? What difference would it make?"

"The difference is that with a supernova, we could go courageously—a noble death. At least we'd know we hadn't designed it, built it, and then—realizing the consequences—gone ahead and used it."

"You know what the generals would say, of course. They'd defend their weapons. They'd say, 'What are you going to do, let Russia overrun the world?'"

"And I'd say right back to them, what are *you* going to do? Bomb the earth in order to save it?

Either way it's a risk. I know that. Nobody can really guarantee what will happen, they can only guess. But I think I'd take my chances with the guys who want to do away with nuclear weapons, who wouldn't use them regardless of what anybody else did. Even if Russia struck first, Dan, I wouldn't want to bomb their cities—kill a lot of kids and old folks." Bill leaned forward, his face earnest. "You know what we need? A new explorer, a new Columbus."

"Yeah?"

"Really. For hundreds of years, you know, people had some strange ideas about the world. Until Columbus and Magellan. For centuries people thought the earth was the center of the universe. Until Copernicus and Galileo. And today, see, we still think in terms of war or surrender. If you can't work things out at the conference table, you fight. If you're not top dog, number one, you're going to end up slaves. People just accept that this is true. I don't think that it is. We need a new explorer to come up with alternatives. That's where Columbus comes in."

Bill held his hands out in front of him suddenly, examining his palms. "Look. Sweat. I really get worked up over this. It's going to be my first editorial for the paper. I was trying it out on you."

"Well, it's original—for our paper, anyway. A lot more profound than writing about new band uniforms or something."

"It makes me feel I'm doing *something,* that's all. That's the only way I can deal with it. *Do* something.

Get involved. Even if the chances are small, at least I'll know I was one of the ones who tried. That's what keeps me going."

Dan thought again of Orlenda. What had she to do with wars and killing? What did she know of the earth or sun or the supernova, 500 million years overdue? All she had wanted from life was to get to the land beyond Deva with her sister and had turned in desperation to Dan for help. His mind wandered, and when he focused on Bill again, his friend was saying,

"So I've got my editorial, I've got a photo story for the sports page, I've got an article on the school board members who are up for reelection, but we need that special travel feature. Can I count on it by August thirtieth, Dan? Would you send it directly to Judith so she can lay it out?"

Dan could not answer that. He could promse nothing. He had other promises to keep. "I don't know," he said finally. "I just don't know."

He should have felt guilty, he decided later as he listened to Bill turning the Buick around in the clearing and heading back toward the road. Bill had taken the better part of a day and a couple gallons of gas to drive down here to see if he was all right, and Dan had enjoyed his company but given nothing in return. He was in no condition, at this point, to be feature editor next year, and Bill would do well to appoint someone else. He was not even sure he would be going back to school. The pleasure he had felt earlier at Bill's visit seemed to be evaporating.

Blossom stood in the doorway behind him.

"He's gone, then?"

"He has a job at a car wash, Bee. Had to be back by four."

She waited. "It would do you good to have more friends about, Dan. Too lonesome down here for a lad your age."

"I've got plenty to do," Dan said, getting up, avoiding her eyes. "Please don't worry about me, Bee. It doesn't help."

HE WAS CONCERNED, once again, about his mind. He found himself driving down Mt. Joy Pike, passing the cemetery at Market Square and Lumber Streets, forgetting why he had come.

He had to make a conscious effort, relive the events of the morning step by step, before he remembered the piece of screen he had planned to purchase. Again the thought surfaced that perhaps he was no longer capable of distinguishing reality from imaginings—that the footsteps and faces and voices that seemed to catch him unaware were products of his own mind, and that it had already begun a process of slow deterioration. The sinking feeling struck once more in the center of his chest, and then he remembered that others had seen and heard things too: Joe Stanton had seen the soldiers, and Blossom had seen the face in the water. As for the footprints outside the parlor window, they were still there, made in the damp earth of evening and sunbaked the following day. If Blossom had noticed, she said nothing.

He purchased the piece of screen mechanically and headed back home. As he parked at the farmhouse, he saw Blossom waiting for him at the front door.

"Ten minutes earlier, and you would have seen him," she said. "A sight he was, too, with gray hair down to his shoulders, a band about his head with a trinket on it, a chain about his neck. . . ."

Dan paused there on the lawn. "Who, Bee?"

"A gypsy. I tried to delay him, knowing you'd be back before long. Such a face you never saw—the black brows, the gray beard—the very way my great-grandfather looked, I would think. But he wouldn't stay, was impatient to be off."

"What happened? What did he want?" Dan came slowly up the steps.

"Came asking if I had any old coins to sell. Said he was a buyer of silver. I offered to sell my old silver butter dish, but it was coins he wanted."

Dan automatically felt for the Roman denarius embedded in the wide band of his watch, tracing the outline of it with his finger. It must have been Ambrose—his description exactly. So he had come, then, while Dan was gone. And it was the Faws who were camped in the woods beyond the south pasture, or the Dawsons, as they now called themselves. So why hadn't Lonnie been back to work? Why were they hiding there in the woods, keeping to themselves?

He shivered as he thought over the events of the day—the visit from Bill, the swim in the creek, the long discussion on the back porch. All the while, from somewhere off in the trees, Ambrose had been watching. And when Dan had driven off later toward town, the old gypsy had come to the house, hoping somehow to trick Bee into finding the coin for him.

Time was getting short. If Ambrose had come once while Dan was gone, he would come again, possibly in the night. Dan wanted to be in control of the situation when they met, wanted to head off a surprise meeting. He would wait no longer. Tonight he would seek them out.

"I got the piece of screen for the attic," he said to Bee, and went on upstairs. At the window of his room he stopped, hands resting on the sill, and looked out over the south pasture. There was no sign of the gypsy now, no trace of smoke. But just beyond the far fence, in the shadow of the walnut grove, stood a gray horse, tethered to a tree, its head down—waiting.

HE WOULD TAKE NOTHING with him when he left—no clothes, no food, but mentally he was preparing for a long trip. He did not know whether he would be back at all. He gave no thought to his parents, to school, to his grandmother, other than his immediate obligations to see that the day's work had been done. He felt feverish, somewhat out of his head. Sounds seemed to jumble together in his ears, questions tumbled over each other without answers. He would start to speak and then forget what he wanted to say, and all the while Blossom watched him—concerned, silent.

Dan came downstairs after washing up and found her starting their supper.

"I really don't want anything to eat, Bee. If I'm hungry later, I'll get something cold from the refrigerator."

"Well, then. . . ." She put down the turnip she had picked up to peel and watched him buttoning his shirt. "Looks like you're going out."

"Thought I'd take a walk—clear my head. Maybe I'll hike back into the woods. I'd like to meet the gypsies before they move on." When Blossom gave no response, Dan asked, "What are they like? You said they've been through before."

"Well now, no two are the same, you know. Sometimes it's just an old man and woman traveling along by themselves—a horse and cart and a tent. Sometimes it's more like a wagon with a makeshift top. And sometimes it's a van. But they all camp out, do their cooking under the stars, and wash their clothes in the stream."

She sighed and let her hands drop in her lap, leaning back in her chair. "There've been times in the past—times when things were going poorly around here, with Thomas the way he was and me not knowing what was wrong with him—when I'd walk to the end of the pasture and go off in the woods a ways. It would be about dusk, just like it is now, and I'd hear music—fiddles, maybe—laughter, talk. All I needed to go join them, I swear it, was a push. But I had me Brian and Shirley then, you see, and a husband, sick or not, so I stayed. But I can tell you that those summers after the gypsies had gone—the music and the smoke from their fires along with them—that I'd feel like a bit of my heart had been taken too. Oh, it's all bosh, I know. You can't get rid of troubles by running away from them; they just follow along behind, that's all. But don't think I wouldn't have liked to try. Oh, my, but I would have liked to!"

"Well, I'll go see for myself," Dan said.

"They're not like the migrants, now," Bee warned. "Some folks, you know, you can start a conversation with easy-like. The migrants I could ask where they'd worked the last and what they were best at doing, and they'd tell it out straight—how many bushels of tomatoes or beans they could pick and what the weather was like in New York state—everyday sort of talk. And if I had me a warm sweater that my children had outgrown or any of Thomas' pants too tight about the middle, why I could just put them in a paper sack and give it to 'em at the end of the day along with their wages and they'd be right grateful. But you don't do that with gypsies."

She saw no connection, then, between the disappearance of Lonnie and the coming of the gypsies, Dan thought.

"No, sir, the gypsies don't want you to know where they've been or where they're going, and if I put a sack of old clothes at the edge of their camp, it would still be sitting there after they'd left. They never did take kindly to handouts, or folks wandering around asking questions. If they want something of yours, they'll take it themselves."

"I'd still like to go," Dan said, and put his hand on the screen.

"I figured you would. Not much excitement around here, that's a fact. Too bad you don't have any old coins to sell. Now that would make you welcome right off."

"Well, we'll see," Dan said, and went out.

He knew that she was standing at the door watching him leave. He could feel her eyes upon him as he opened the gate to the south pasture. But as soon as he was out of sight behind the barn, he forgot all that lay behind him.

3

DUSK TOOK OVER the south pasture. The horse wandered up to the barn, the cow following along behind, as though some unseen keeper had called them home. The crickets picked up where the birds left off, and occasionally a firefly sparkled above the tall grass—now here, now there —like a will-o'-the-wisp luring Dan on toward the forest.

With each step he took, the distant trees seemed to grow a deeper shade of blue-gray until at last, after he had swung himself over the fence and entered the walnut grove—prelude to the woods beyond, darkness fell quickly.

Now and then he startled a bird out of hiding, and with a sudden flutter of wings, the creature darted from the underbrush and into the trees above. Dan had thought he'd been going in the direction of the smoke, beyond the place where Blossom's stream merged with the waters of Little Donegal Creek. But now, as he scanned the path with his flashlight, he could not judge exactly how far he had come or how far there was to go.

He stopped, relying on his other senses, listening for the sound of a fiddle that Bee had talked about, testing the air with his nostrils for the onion-rabbit stew he had eaten once on the moor.

He had no doubt that Lonnie's family and the gypsies were one. Yet the young man had not responded to the name Jasper, had not seemed to know what Dan was talking about when he mentioned the moor. Was it possible that Lonnie's father, the Andrew Dawson who traveled the banks of the Susquehanna with his brood, following the seasons, was another form, another version, of Ambrose Faw? And was it conceivable, even, that the Ambrose Faw he had met outside York on his trip last spring was a ghostly reincarnation of the Brigante chieftain of the fourth century? Whether either man was aware of his past in Roman Britain except through occasional swatches of dreams, strangely remembered scenes, Dan didn't know. It was beyond explaining, but he felt sure that, whether Dawsons or Faws, they were all travelers, born somehow of a river, spawned in the sea, and that the Lonnie whom Bee had hired earlier that summer was actually Jasper Faw.

There was movement in the bushes to his left, and Dan turned, catching a young man in the beam of his flashlight. He startled as he recognized the face —most certainly that of Nat, Orlenda's younger brother, who had traded him the denarius in exchange for Dan's belt. It was an older Nat, however, than he had known last spring on the moor—now a year older than Dan, perhaps. But as Dan opened his mouth to speak to him, the young man disappeared, and the leaves closed in behind him, filling the space, as though he had not been there at all.

Dan stood rooted to the spot, looking about him, puzzled. If this was indeed the same gypsy family he had met in England, then Nat was Gabe, as Lonnie had called him, and Orlenda was Oriole. Yet if Gabe had gone off to join the army, as Lonnie had said, why was he back?

Slowly Dan went on, not wanting to startle the gypsies, trying to let the twigs snap naturally under his feet, making no sudden movements. When he could make out the yellow glow of a campfire up ahead, he began to whistle, forcing his legs into a casual stroll.

"Anybody here?" he called when he was in sight of the clearing.

An old green truck stood off to one side. It was a makeshift affair—the fenders of a different vintage, and an entire door that had been replaced with one of red. It was smaller than a delivery truck, larger than a van—more like a school bus, actually, except that there were fewer windows.

Those that remained had curtains on them, each of a different pattern, and silhouetted against the warm yellow light from inside was a small pot of African violets that looked almost black under the night sky.

The gray horse that Dan had seen from his bedroom window was grazing beside the truck. And watching from the open door were two girls, the younger sitting, the older standing.

"I've come to see Mr. Dawson," Dan called from the edge of the trees, taking a chance that the name would fit.

A woman he had not noticed before hunching over a fire slowly raised herself and stared at him, the cooking spoon motionless in her hand.

Then, from around the truck, came the gypsy. The eyes were even more fierce than Dan had remembered. The heavy jowls, the gray-black mustache above the lip, the beard that flowed wild and unruly down upon the mammoth chest—a bear of a man in a checked shirt and old pants, the trousers of a suit that had long been separated from the jacket.

"Hello," Dan repeated, for the gypsy had stopped and was looking at him without moving, his eyes squinting, as though deciding what to do. . . .

Dan took a tentative step forward.

"My grandmother said you came by this afternoon while I was out. Said you were a buyer of silver coins. I thought I'd walk over."

The crinkles around the gypsy's eyes deepened.

"Ah! Stay and have a sup with us, then," he said jovially, coming over and extending a hand. "Andrew Dawson, that's my name."

So he was right.

"Dan Roberts. Lonnie was working at our farm before he left."

"It was your farm, then," Andrew Dawson motioned toward a log on the ground. "Come on, come on, have a sit-down. This is the wife, Reba . . ." He turned slightly. ". . . and Oriole, there in the doorway, and little Nancy. . . ."

"Hello," Dan said again, and sat. It was difficult not to look at Oriole, not to go to her immediately. But he waited.

Lonnie had come up from the stream with a bucket of water and stopped, staring, when he saw Dan. He glanced quickly at his father.

"It's good to see you, Lonnie," Dan said, hoping to put him at ease.

Lonnie nodded briefly.

"I saw Gabe as I was coming in," Dan continued, wanting to keep it open and honest.

The family seemed to freeze in their places. Reba looked at her husband. Everyone, it seemed, was watching Andrew.

"Well, then, you've met us all," the gypsy said, recovering quickly, a false cheerfulness in his voice. And speaking, it seemed, to the trees, he called, "Come on, Gabe, and eat with us."

The young man came out of the shadows and over to the fire. His hair was cropped short like that of a military recruit, and despite the warmth of the evening, he seemed chilled, and sat bent over, hugging himself with his arms.

His father watched with seeming amusement.

"When a gypsy is cold," he said to Dan, "he sits huddled up like a wet hen. But when the fire gets going, you can watch his feathers expand."

Dan was convinced it was fear, more than cold, that had overwhelmed Gabe, and he studied the young man across from him. As Gabe straightened up finally, however, Dan caught a glimpse of something shiny at his waist, and when he looked more closely, he saw the belt buckle—the brass eagle—gleaming in the glow of the fire.

IT WAS LIKE being in the Faws' camp for the first time on the moor: the silences, the stares, the gestures, and the eyes—like dark olives—watching. Sometimes when Dan looked at Oriole, she looked away, yet it was Orlenda, surely. Other times it was she who was doing the watching. And all the while Lonnie sat off by himself, embarrassed, it seemed, that Dan had come, had found them here.

"I was needed back with the family," he said to Dan by way of explanation. "Looked like any day we could be moving on."

"That's okay," Dan said. "We'll be hiring someone else."

Like Gabe, the other family members were older than the ones he had known in York, It was as though time had speeded up and he was five years off in the future. The father's hair was more gray than black, the mother's face more lined, like that of the old granny's now, with tiny creases above and below the lips. Lonnie was twenty-four or twenty-five, Oriole in her early twenties, Gabe seventeen, and Nancy, the youngest, a child of seven.

The meal was served on tin plates, hot to the touch, and Dan set his on the grass to cool. Again it crossed his mind that he had done the same on the moor.

"Eat! Eat!" Andrew Dawson said, his mouth full, motioning to Dan's plate with the loaf of bread he held in one hand. He broke off a piece and passed it on. "It's good to have company. So you are also a dealer in coins?"

Dan picked up his plate again and tried resting it on his lap. "It depends," he said.

The gypsy's eyes narrowed and he began to smile —a slow smile, his lips widening until Dan could see the gleam of his gold tooth. "Depends, eh? A bargainer, that's what you be, eh? Well, I like a shrewd businessman, I do. Do you trade or do you sell?"

Dan hesitated, not wanting to play his hand too quickly. He needed time to talk with Oriole. He could not end the evening so soon. "Sometimes I only buy," he said at last.

The smile disappeared from Andrew's face. He went on eating silently, but did not take his eyes from Dan. Even when a dollop of rice and beans dropped down onto his shirt, the dark eyes remained fixed.

The bread traveled around the group, from hand to hand. Gabe passed it to Dan, their eyes met for a moment, and again Dan glanced at the belt with the eagle buckle, its beak forming the prong. How was it possible there could be such a coincidence? Most certainly it was the very belt he had traded three months ago in York.

"That's an interesting belt," Dan told him. "Did you get it around here?"

Gabe smiled slightly.

"About," he answered.

"You'd trade for the belt?" Andrew Dawson said from across the fire, the crinkles beginning around the eyes again. And when Dan hesitated, he said, "It's a fine belt—a buckle that will last forever."

"I don't know," said Dan, and then to Gabe, "What would you take for it?"

Gabe looked at his father but did not reply.

Andrew Dawson leaned forward. "It's a very good belt, an excellent buckle," he continued as though he hadn't heard. "You can find no more like it anywhere. An antique, that's what it is."

"What would you want for it?" Dan repeated.

"A foreign coin," the gypsy said. "Something very old—something worthy of the belt."

The silence in the camp was awful. There seemed to be no sound at all—no breeze, no whisper, no breath. The gypsies sat with hands poised above their plates, mouths unmoving. All eyes were watching.

"Like a Roman denarius?" Dan said.

The very words seemed to make the Dawsons tremble, as though an ill-wind had risen up out of the ground and gone swirling among them. Dan half-expected to be seized, thrown on his back, and the denarius to be taken from him by force.

"Yes, a Roman denarius," the gypsy repeated, his eyes small, like two burning coals in the darkness, and he said nothing more.

"I'll have to think about it," Dan told him and continued eating.

For a full minute it seemed as though he were eating alone, surrounded by an audience. No gesture of his hands, no sound of his lips escaped them. Faking unconcern, he lifted a piece of meat to his mouth again, and then slowly the family came to life and the meal continued as before.

"Music!" the gypsy said suddenly. "Music!"

"Lonnie's the fiddler," Gabe said, motioning his head toward his older brother.

Oriole spoke then for the first time, and Dan studied her face, hoping for some sign of recognition: "You play, Lonnie, and Mother will sing."

"Not tonight," said Reba, the worry lines etched in her face. "There are too many things on my mind."

"Then we will have the fiddle without the singing," said the gypsy, and Lonnie got up reluctantly and went into the truck, returning with the instrument.

Dan was glad for the distraction, for a chance to pull himself together and decide what to do. He was drinking something that Andrew Dawson had poured in his cup, something that tasted like cider.

He remembered the drink he had been served on the moor and what had happened after that. He decided to drink nothing else. He would need all his wits about him this night.

Finally, as the music slowed and then stopped, Dan wondered how long he should stay, how long he could politely prolong his visit. They had given him dinner and soon he would be required either to say his goodbye or make an offer for the belt. He had hoped to talk with Oriole alone before he left. When he saw her gathering up the plates and the cooking pot, he quickly offered to carry the kettle down to the stream for her. And the gypsy, watching from the shadows, let him go.

As HE FOLLOWED her down through the gully, he felt increasingly awkward. What would he say that would not scare her off? Ask if she had known him in another time and place? What could he say that would not make him sound like a raving lunatic? *Oriole,* he repeated to himself, not wanting to make a mistake. *Her name is Oriole.* He went on, following her swinging gait as she moved down the path, her skirt swishing, a lantern in one hand and the stack of plates in the other.

The problem was resolved when, once they were away from camp, the girl turned abruptly and faced him.

"Did you come about Gabe?" she asked, almost defiantly, yet there was a tremor in her voice.

Dan tried to put together the pieces, to understand what it was she was asking.

"I want to help in any way that I can," he said simply.

Gradually her face seemed to relax, to soften, and finally her shoulders slumped with relief. Orlenda's eyes most certainly—Orlenda's lips, the curve of her neck. . . .

"I've been so frightened," she said, and began walking again, this time beside him. "Any moment I expect an officer to come after him. When I heard you coming through the underbrush, I told myself that if it was a soldier come for my brother, I would throw myself in front of him. He would have to shoot me before he could take Gabe back."

There could be only one explanation, Dan decided; Gabe had deserted. What had happened once at the end of the fourth century was happening again now. It was as though he were destined to play this scene again and again, as though he, who faced an uncertainty all his own, could move swiftly, easily, into the lives of others whose futures were also tenuous.

"How long has he been back?" Dan asked.

"Only a few days. It happened when we were camped across the river. We left so quickly we scarcely had time to put out the cooking fire. When Gabe came back, we hid with him all afternoon beneath an old bridge, back behind the railroad tracks, and crossed the river in the middle of the night. Gabe said they would send someone looking. They always do."

"They did."

She jerked her head quickly, pausing to stare at him, suddenly tense.

"I went to Mt. Wolf that afternoon looking for you, not Gabe," Dan explained. "Lonnie had told me about your family, and I thought you might need me, I'm not sure why. I asked an old man in an antique store if he knew where you camped. He said that someone else had been there that very morning asking about you, and he wanted to make sure I was really a friend."

"Who was it that had come looking?"

"A man, a brash man, he put it."

"What did he tell him?"

"He said that you had already come and gone and were heading down the river toward the Bay."

Oriole's eyes grew wider at first, then smaller as she began to smile.

"To me, he told the truth," Dan went on. "I went to the place where you had camped—in the pine trees beyond the cemetery—and you had gone, but there were still red coals among the ashes of your fire. I'm curious how Lonnie found you. My grandmother let him go early that day, I discovered later, because of the storm."

"We had to leave a sign," Oriole said simply, and Dan remembered the *patrin*, the gypsy arrangement of sticks that tells other relatives the direction in which they have gone.

He wanted somehow to convey to her that he had known her before, that he knew about gypsy customs. So he said, "On my way back to the car that day, I found an unmarked grave at the edge of the cemetery. There was a thorn bush planted there and, wound about in its branches, a faded piece of red yarn."

She looked at him strangely, her eyebrows arched, waiting.

"I was afraid when I saw it that something might have happened in your family," Dan told her, "that something might have happened to you."

"But it's an old grave," she protested.

"You know it, then—the one I'm talking about."

She stared at him curiously. "Yes, I know the grave. We buried Granny there several years ago. And it was I who threaded the yarn through the branches. How did you connect it to us? Did Lonnie tell you?"

"No. It was just a feeling I had that I'd known your family before. It's crazy, I suppose. . . ."

She seemed to accept that, and laughed a little.

"No. Granny wouldn't think so. Granny was always seeing things—people—from somewhere else. Soldiers. That's what she saw. She told me once."

Dan chose his words carefully. "I see them too now and then. Roman soldiers."

"I don't know what kind Granny saw, but to me they're all alike. I hate them all."

They reached the stream in the gully. Oriole

knelt down on the edge of the bank and began swishing the tin plates in the water, rubbing at them with the palm of her hand, then scraping at the sticky places with her knuckles.

"Set the pot in the water and let it soak awhile," she instructed.

Dan was glad for a reason to linger, and quietly watched the bubbles rise to the surface when the large pot went in.

"What will your family do now?" he asked, sitting down on the bank and resting his arms on his knees. Oriole faced him, the lantern between them, and tucked her feet under the hem of her long red skirt. Her eyes had a sad sort of sparkle.

"We'll hide here with Gabe until it's time to take him to Canada. We can think of nothing else."

"How can you be sure that's the answer? He could be stopped at the border. What will he live on once he's there?"

"My father has a plan. If Gabe has his pockets full of American money, he says, he'll be discovered and sent back home. So we're looking for foreign coins to give him instead. When we have enough, and Gabe's hair has grown longer, we'll slip him across the border at night. In the morning, he can find a coin shop and sell his collection for Canadian money. That way no one will suspect. My father, you see, is very clever."

Dan was silent for a time. A desperate plan by a desperate family. He could tell by the pitch of her voice that the girl was nervous, eager for his approval, frantic for reassurance that the plan would work.

"Then what, Oriole? You'll be separated from him, and Gabe will always fear that he might be found out. He'll have no legal papers, no friends, and you'll worry about him just the same."

As soon as he said it, he wished he had not, for Oriole buried her face on her knees, her slim brown arms wrapped tightly about her legs, rocking herself slightly from side to side. When she raised her face at last, there seemed to be lines that had not been there before, creases that had sprung up mysteriously about the mouth. She looked old before her time, and yet she was still Oriole—still, in fact, Orlenda.

"Do you know what you have to do to be a good soldier, Dan? To be a good soldier you have to hate. You have to hate someone you don't even know. Someone that—if there weren't a war—you might like to walk beside in the woods, or fish beside in the streams, or sit beside when you play your guitar. The day Gabe discovered this was the day they gave him a bayonet. And he had to run up to a straw man—a bag filled with hay—and drive the bayonet through to the other side." She leaned back against the trunk of a tree, shivered almost imperceptibly, and then went on.

"The sergeant made fun of Gabe. He said he might as well shake hands with the dummy he was being so polite about it. And all the men were laughing. He made Gabe do it again and again, and each time it was never right. Gabe drove the bayonet in the straw, but it was never fast enough or hard enough or deep enough or...the truth is...vicious enough.

"And so the sergeant gave the dummy a name— 'Charlie,' he called it. He swore at Charlie and kicked him and made up stories about him. He said that Charlie was out to kill Gabe's mother and rape his sisters, and he told Gabe to think about these things when he ran with the bayonet—to bare his teeth like an animal and growl in his throat, to curse at the straw man there on the pole and to shout when he drove the bayonet through. And that was when Gabe learned about hating—about how it's supposed to be in the army. As long as he thought of the enemy as someone like himself—unsure and confused—he just couldn't help feeling sorry."

She absently toyed with the lantern, turning it around and around on the grass, sending eerie shadows dancing about from one tree trunk to another.

" 'Who will we be fighting?' Gabe would ask the sergeant. 'Tell me who they are and what they've done to us, and perhaps I can get angry.' And the sergeant would say, 'Why, it could be anyone at all— the Russians, the Chinese, the Arabs, the Turks. . . .' 'I can't hate them all,' Gabe would tell him. And the sergeant would answer, 'You'll learn.' And finally, when Gabe said he didn't think he would ever learn, the sergeant told him he didn't even have to think about it; all he had to do was follow orders."

Oriole looked at Dan earnestly. "It sounds so honorable, doesn't it? So fine. . . . Obeying orders. I wonder how many horrible things have been done in the world just by obeying orders."

"And yet, if there was no one in charge, if we all just did what we wanted to. . . ."

"I know. I've thought of that, too. Gabe finally went to the chaplain to tell him how he felt. The chaplain said that maybe Gabe could think of war as a 'horrible necessity.' That's what he said, Dan, a horrible necessity—that might prevent something even more horrible later on."

"He might be right."

"Yes, he might. But also, he might not. It might even lead to something more horrible. If people do awful things because they might prevent something even worse, it excuses almost anything, doesn't it? That is the worst evil of all, doing awful things and pretending all the while that you are really brave and good. How much simpler it is when conscience and duty agree."

"And so Gabe deserted."

"Yes." Oriole sighed deeply. "Mother said she knew it would happen; that very morning, in fact, she said it."

"How did she know?"

Oriole shrugged. "She began to shiver. It was after Lonnie had gone off to work and Father had just come back from driving him. 'It's something about Gabe,' Mother said, and took to bed she was shivering so. And we didn't go to the lettuce fields because of her, but waited to see if a fever would follow. And minutes later Gabe came through the brush, covered with burrs, his face dirty, his clothes torn. 'They'll be sending someone after me,' he told us, and in ten minutes we had picked up camp and hidden the truck."

A sadness seemed to well up inside Dan, a certainty that Oriole was going to be hurt and disappointed, that someone should protect her from this.

"So Gabe is going to be hidden, coming out at night like an animal, afraid for himself, afraid for you. . . . That's no way to live, Oriole."

Her eyes filled quickly with tears, which hung there for a moment, then spilled out. "There's nothing else, Dan! There's just nothing else." She covered her face with her hands and cried. Dan reached forward and touched her arm, wishing desperately that somehow he might comfort her. He was miserable watching her weep.

"I don't know. It seems to me that our country ought to be big enough to find a place for people like Gabe, who feel the way he does. Who knows who's really right?" He remembered an article that Bill had written last year for the school paper—a piece on draft registration and conscientious objectors. He tried to remember what Bill had said. "Listen, Oriole. There are places Gabe can go—where anyone can go or write—if he feels the way Gabe feels about war. There's one in Philadelphia. They'll counsel him so that he can decide what to do."

"They'd turn him in."

"No, I'm sure they wouldn't."

"He would go to prison."

"I don't think so. They might fight his case for him so that he doesn't have to run away. Maybe they can find something useful for him to do so he could serve his country in another way."

"He would be ridiculed, Dan. Men would say he was a coward."

"Would it have been more honorable for Gabe to stay, Oriole, feeling as he does? Would he have been true to himself?"

She looked at Dan intently, and there was something deeper in her eyes that had not been there before. "You sound like a very kind person, Dan. I think you really understand. . . ."

"I understand about feeling trapped," he told her. "Feeling that something terrible is hanging over you and that somehow you can't escape."

"What has happened that makes you understand this?"

"It's a long story. Perhaps sometime I'll tell it to you."

SHE RETURNED to washing the pot in the stream, rubbing at it with a pinecone. Dan watched her and sensed that she was glad he had come, content to have him there beside her.

"Does the name 'Orlenda' mean anything to you?" he asked finally.

She stopped rubbing for a moment. "Orlenda?"

"You've never heard the name before? It's a girl's name."

"I'm not sure. Perhaps . . . long ago." There seemed to be a struggle in her face, as though she were dredging up something long forgotten. She shook her head suddenly, as though to clear it of confusion, and continued her work.

Why was it that only he could remember, Dan wondered—that only he could make the connections?

"I wish I could stay here," Oriole said. "I wish we could stay back here in this woods forever, and you would come and talk to us and bring us news."

"No, you don't, Oriole. Not really. You wouldn't want to be afraid all the time that something awful would happen. I'll do anything for you that I can, but I'm not sure that hiding will help."

"I'll tell Father what you said about Philadelphia," Oriole said, "but he may not trust you. He only let you come in our camp because you talked of coins."

"But you trust me."

"Yes, that I do, truly."

"Then I'll give you something to repay that trust," Dan said. "I have the coin I was talking about —a Roman denarius. If you feel it's really best that Gabe go to Canada as your father planned, then give the coin to him so that he can sell it there. But if he talks with the counselors in Philadelphia and decides to stay, then I would like you to keep the coin, as a remembrance of me."

She looked at him curiously. "Where is this Roman denarius?"

"I have it here." He unbuckled the thick leather watchband from around his wrist.

Dan knew, even as he did so, that it might be a trick. He knew it was possible that it all had been cunningly arranged, that Oriole had led him here to the water for a purpose, and that both her tale of Gabe's desertion and her tears had been rehearsed. He knew also that once the coin had left his possession, he might lose forever his chance to return to the Orlenda he had once known. But he could not ask for trust if he did not give it in return, and he truly believed in this girl beside him.

Oriole picked up the lantern and leaned closer, holding it up so that the light fell on Dan's fingers as he worked with his watchband. With his thumbnail he picked at the slit in the leather, which he had sealed with epoxy, and at last the edges gave way. Slipping one finger inside, he pushed out the coin and held it there in the palm of his hand.

"Here," he said to the dark-eyed girl. "I won't sell or trade it. It's a gift—to you."

As she leaned forward, holding the lantern close so as to see the coin better, the edge of the hot glass touched Dan's finger. He jerked his hand away instinctively, and as he did so, the coin toppled out of his palm and into the stream.

"No!" Oriole cried desperately, horrified at what she had done. She set the lantern on the bank and thrust both arms into the water, frantically searching the bottom.

Dan felt a numbness in his chest, which spread out toward his shoulders, his back, his brain. To have brought it so far, hidden it so well, and now to have lost the denarius. . . .

"It was so stupid of me!" Oriole wept.

"It must be here," Dan reassured her. He reached down and put his arms in beside hers, searching along the sand. Their fingers touched, then parted, then touched again, and it seemed as though the light in the lantern had suddenly gone out, and that darkness was sucking them in.

4

THROUGH TUNNELS of rock and tunnels of time, through light and dark and birth and death and oceans and oceans around him. Through fever and stench and thirst and then—a sweet, sweet coolness upon his face.

Dan tried to open his eyes, but the lashes were matted together. He slowly raised one hand, rubbing a finger across his sticky lids, and as he did so he felt the strange dryness of his face and the way the skin hung slack.

There was water close by. He could hear it, smell it, sense it, and he leaned forward, reaching out with cupped hands, and brought a splash of it to his face. The lids of his eyes unsealed themselves, sunlight filtered through, and then he saw the girl crouched there before him and knew that it was Orlenda.

"Daniel!" The girl crossed herself, rocking back on her heels, and remained motionless, one hand to her throat. "Surely it's you, and alive, too!"

Had it happened, then? Had the river taken him again, borne upon its ancient currents, into the Roman Britain where he had left the girl once before? He had come all this way to find her, yet was too stunned to speak her name. Something about her was different—her speech, her clothes—and slowly it came to him that this was not the time or the place that he had known her in the past.

As always, he could remember Blossom's farm and all that had gone on there, but had no knowledge of who he was here, or what had happened to him to make the girl stare so. That he was experiencing the past, he felt sure; that it was now his present, that he knew also; but exactly where he was or when. . . . He was seized suddenly with dizziness and dropped his head, closing his eyes.

The girl crept closer but stll did not touch him. He could tell by the sound of her rustlings that she kept herself at a distance.

"Daniel, I can hardly believe this!" she said again, a surprised delight in her voice. "You are so much better than you were. Surely my prayers have saved you."

He had been ill, then. That he could believe. He felt ill. He felt already dead, in fact. Slowly he opened his eyes, with great effort, and waited until they focused on Orlenda. He knew, even before he opened his lips, that his own speech would sound strange to him but not to her.

"What was the sickness?" he asked, at once aware of the terrible taste in his mouth, the stink of his own breath. And then he thought about the words as he had spoken them. English, yet the strangest dialect he had ever heard. He spoke it naturally and well.

"It's no wonder you can't remember, for it's wonder enough you're alive," Orlenda answered. "It was the pestilence, Daniel. We had given you up for dead."

The pestilence, she had said. Dan let his eyes travel down his body. He was indeed thin. His bare feet looked much too big and swollen for his sticklike legs; the skin itself was filthy. Not only his breath but his body stank, and he was embarrassed to have Orlenda see him in such a condition. He turned his head away and raised one arm to cover his face. As he did so, he was conscious of a dull pain beneath the armpit. Feeling there with the other hand, he touched a large scab, sticky and rough. He pulled his hand away quickly in revulsion.

"When we saw the boils that had come upon you, we said, 'He is finished,' " Orlenda told him. "One of Christ's arrows had struck you down. I cried so, Daniel. Mother wouldn't let me come near you, but twice I crept out at night and placed food on your doorstep. I don't know if you found it or if the pigs ate it instead. For many days you didn't come out, and when at last we saw you stagger down toward the river, we felt you had gone there to die, and Father burned your hut to the ground, lest the pestilence spread to us all. God forgive him, but no one knows what to do that will save us."

He stared at her incredulously.

She sighed. "But there were others, we found, who had brought the sickness even before you—an eye doctor, for one, who had passed through only a few days before and was found dead on the road to Chester. Already four people have died, and daily we get news of more who fall ill. Buy you're going to *live*, Daniel! I can tell by your eyes. You're so much better! God is sometimes merciful. May he be so with us."

"Your family?" It was an effort to speak, for his lips were dry and his tongue sticky.

"We are still well. But the great mortality is all about us. Such a beautiful spring, too; such a blueness of sky. And just when the blossoms were at their peak, the sickness came to York."

Dan sat up slowly and gently swung his swollen feet into the river. He was wearing a tunic with vomit stains on the front. Everything stank, as though he had been living intimately with death.

"Tell me all that happened, Orlenda," he said. "My head is still reeling. I'm not myself."

She looked at him cautiously. "You remember nothing?"

"Almost nothing. How did it begin?"

"You are blest, Daniel, not to remember. It was a year ago when we first heard of the pestilence. A peddler came through, who had heard of it from a seaman. A great mortality, he said, was raging far across the water in Italy, people dying every day. And we shook our heads and soon forgot it. The next we heard, it was in France, near the very place where Nat had fought. . . ."

"He was a soldier?"

"So to speak. He went with his master to war. The master came home safe and sound. It was Nat who had a wound in the leg. But the stories we heard, of a place called Avignon, where whole families had died of the pestilence and pits were filled with their bodies! We listened, but still we did not worry. The Continent is far away, the people foreign. And then, in the heat of the summer, the Archbishop of York sent out a warning. A great infection of the air threatened England, he said, caused by the sins of man. And he urged us all to pray, which we have done day and night. By autumn, the pestilence reached our coast."

"Here? Near York?"

"No, no. It was still far from us, in the south of England—in Dorset. But by then, we lived with the constant dread that it would soon be upon us. Every time a traveler came through, we would ask what news he brought, and with each mention of a village or town, we could tell it was creeping closer. And then you came, with the news that the pestilence was in Lincolnshire. . . ."

She drew her knees up to her chest, wrapped her slim arms around them, her feet hidden by her long skirt. "It's a horrible thing to know that something terrible is on its way, Daniel. I wish it had come quickly, without warning, so that I might have been happy until the last."

"Is there nothing the doctors can do?"

She reached up and touched a small bag of herbs

on a string about her neck. "We wear these to keep away the smell of death. We have been told to stay away from the sickly, not to allow travelers into our homes. The bells ring out on every occasion of joy to stir the stagnant air. But still we wait and wonder who will be next."

Orlenda got to her feet and stood looking out over the river. "Father says that York has never been so prosperous. We have our cathedral and our monasteries and a mill, and the wharves are always busy with goods coming and going. And yet, last year—a few days after Christmas—a terrible, terrible flood covered our western parishes. The river rose and rats were everywhere. An omen, Mother said. And now, in such a beautiful spring, there is a stench of death among us. Are things always this way, Daniel, do you suppose? I have been born into the worst of all possible times, truly I have."

He wanted to tell her that she had felt so once before—a long, long time ago. But she would not understand.

THEY CAME SLOWLY up the path from the river to the small plot of land where the house of Orlenda's father stood. It was a mud and wattle cottage, with roof of reeds, and the cooking smoke seeped from every crack and pore. By now the girl had lost her fear of contagion and let Dan lean on her, taking a step at a time and waiting until he had steadied himself.

As they approached the house, however, an old

woman squinting at them from the doorway suddenly rushed out, picked up a stick, and began beating her granddaughter about the shoulders, screaming, "Stupid girl! Have you lost your senses? You bring the pestilence upon us all!"

Orlenda's mother and younger sister appeared then in the doorway, and the mother, too, gave a shriek.

"It is passed, Mother. It's passed!" Orlenda cried out. "Look! His boils have broken and healed over."

The granny stopped beating at her and edged around in front to stare at Dan's face, still keeping her distance. Rose, the mother, came down the path.

"It's true, then," the mother said, looking Dan over carefully as he stood tottering there amid the pigs and chickens, held up only by the strong young woman beside him. "God struck you and spared you at the same time, Daniel; few others have lived to see such a day." And then, turning to Orlenda, she said, "Where will he go, daughter? Ambrose has burned his hut."

The granny began to cluck and chatter, and the little girl chimed in. It was finally decided that Dan should have the ramshackle shed by the side of the house. The pig that had been rooting about inside was chased away, a few armfuls of straw were scattered about, and at last Dan was able to lower himself to the ground. He sprawled, half sitting, in the doorway and drank the gruel that Rose brought to him. Rachel, the small daughter, peeped at him shyly from time to time, but Dan could hardly muster the strength to smile. When the gruel was gone, he set the bowl outside, laid himself down full length, and slept.

He awoke when the angle of sun reached his eyelids, and judged it to be late afternoon. Rachel sat just outside the doorway, clutching a doll made of rags in one hand and drawing designs in the earth with a stick. She stopped and looked at him as he sat up, and when he asked if he could have water, she jumped up and went scampering off.

It was not Rachel who brought the water, but Ambrose. Dan could tell, even with his eyes closed, that a huge shadow had crossed the doorway. He opened them to see a giant of a man standing there with a flask in his hand, his skin the color of old mahogany. He was dressed in a coarse brown tunic, patched several times over, and smelled of sweat and earth and fresh manure. His graying hair hung long about his shoulders, and his beard flowed down onto his chest, spreading out in all directions.

For a moment he stood there in the doorway, his face shadowed, his muscular arms motionless. Then finally he reached down, setting the flask on the earth with one calloused hand, and stood up again, towering above Dan.

"I didn't think, when I burned your hut, that you would ever be back," he said.

The words seemed simply a statement, not an apology. What had they been to each other before?

Dan wondered. Friends? Neighbors only? His throat was too dry to respond, so he lifted the flask to his lips and drank—slowly at first, then more greedily, welcoming the coolness of the water. When he sat the flask down, he said, "Well, what had I to lose but my bed and the roof over me? I've a bed and roof here."

Rose appeared beside her husband then.

"Your pens and ink, lad, and all your parchment," she said in answer. "All of that is gone. Not one of us expected you to come back, for you looked like death itself. Where you have kept yourself all this time, I don't know."

Dan tried to take in what she was telling him. Pen, ink, parchment? Was he a writer, perhaps? He leaned back against the wall and tried to focus his mind on the dates of the Black Death as he remembered them from a history class. The fourteenth century, he felt sure.

Rose took the flask and disappeared once more, leaving only the figure of Ambrose behind. There was something more, it seemed, that he wanted to say.

"There was no malice in it," he said finally, ". . . in the burning. Not a thing did I take for myself, nor did I allow any of my family to go inside."

Dan shrugged. "There was nothing much to take, it seems."

"We will get you pens again if you've need of them," the man repeated. Then he turned and lumbered away. A few yards from the shed, almost hidden from view, he turned once again and stood looking back over his shoulder, then moved on.

DAN DRIFTED IN and out of sleep—awakened by flies that lit on his face, lulled to unconsciousness again by his own exhaustion. He could not separate his thoughts from his dreams. He had come once more to Orlenda at a time of great danger. He envisioned himself leading her family to safety, taking them up into the hills where the plague could not touch them. He reveled at the gratitude they would show him, the look in Orlenda's eyes, and for a time he almost believed it was happening. Like the gypsy Faws he had known in York, they would move along the road in a colorful procession, their belongings heaped in a cart. Some would ride in the wagon, the others would go on horseback. He and Orlenda, of course, would ride together, and he would feel her head against his chest, her hair against his cheek. . . . He smiled in his sleep at his own imaginings.

When he woke again, the procession had vanished, but the resolution remained: he must get the family away from York as quickly as possible; as soon as he had recovered, he must persuade them to leave. If they had no cart, he would build one. If they had no horses, he would borrow them. If there wasn't enough food to make the journey, they would get whatever they could along the way.

He brushed the flies off once more and rolled over on his side. If only his strength would return, if only his body were well. . . .

As laborers returned home from the markets and workers from the fields, there were more visitors to the shed. Standing a safe distance from the doorway, they congregated in little groups of three or four, straining their necks to see Dan. At first they kept their voices to a whisper, but as each group left and another took its place, the message was spoken aloud—from farmer to fishmonger, from laundress to butcher: "Daniel the Young, the Scribe, has recovered. By the Lord's grace," they said, "he's been healed. It's a miracle!"

"A miracle! A miracle!" The news traveled on. "The yellow's gone from his eyes. The swellings are down."

Dan felt fatigued and was embarrassed by the attention. He crept back further into the shed, away from the doorway, but it was warm and the place smelled of pigs, nauseating him. Orlenda came in at that moment carrying one of her brothers' tunics. Shoes had been found for him also—soft leather slippers, handsewn.

"The bells rang for you, Daniel. Did you hear them?" she said as she helped put them over his swollen feet. "The butcher told us. There was a crier, too, telling it in the streets. York rejoices that you live."

Dan was still too exhausted to care much. He realized that his recovery had brought hope, however, for if God could spare one, the people must reason, might not He spare them all?

It was Nat who brought Dan's supper, a modest meal of cheese and bread and ale. He placed it on the floor of the shed and lowered himself to the ground, one leg stiffly out in front of him.

He was not quite the young boy Dan remembered from the gypsy camp, the boy who had badgered him to trade his belt for the Roman denarius. Nor was he the agitated recruit hiding in the woods behind Blossom's farm. His face looked youthful, as though his eyes denied what he had seen abroad and his ears shut out what he had heard. But his stiff leg, like that of an old man, made him wince as he tried to find a position that was comfortable.

"I'm not myself," Dan told him. "I know you, and yet I don't. I remember almost nothing of what went before. How long have I been ill?"

Nat slowly rubbed his leg and studied Dan. "You were abed when we found you, so I don't know how long before that. You were as close to death as a man can come without being buried."

"I was a scribe, then?"

"You remember nothing of that? You were a peddlar scribe. You had no shop or table or chair, but carried your pens and parchment on your back and traveled here by foot. You wrote letters for the common folk and sent them off with any traveler heading for the place the letters were to go. Sometimes, when you moved on, you told us, you carried some of the letters yourself."

"Yet I had a house here in York?"

"It wasn't yours. It was a hut once used by the pig keeper, and when he died it was left standing, too foul smelling for human use. But age and time and the wind blowing through the cracks had cleared it, I suppose. In any case, when you came by, you took it as your own, and there was no one to stop you and few who cared."

"I did nothing else for a living but write letters?"

"With the pestilence coming, there are many people in want of a scribe. Everyone asks about a friend or a brother in the villages south of York. Everyone wants to send a warning or a message to someone in the towns to the north. It is an awful thing, Daniel. The archbishop urges us to pray and to join in processions of penitence. But the processions seem to do us no good, or the doctors' purgings, either. If all the learned men of York cannot stop it, can you blame my father for burning your hut?"

"No, I don't blame him. It may have been a wise thing. Have we been friends for a while, then?"

Nat looked at him curiously. "It's a wonder you have no memory of this, Daniel."

"It's as though I were never here at all," Dan said truthfully. "Were we friends?"

"We gave you meat and milk when we had it to spare, and Orlenda took you the first berries of the season."

Dan watched him closely. "But we weren't friends?"

Nat hesitated. "You came at the wrong time, Daniel. You were welcome and you weren't. At first we were eager to talk to all travelers. The sickness was something far away, and the stories we heard were awesome. But as we learned of the high contagion of this disease, we began to resent anyone passing through. It was said that the very breath of an afflicted person brought on death—his look, even. Yet people continued to come—merchants, traveling doctors, peddlers, men of the sea, and there was little we could do to stop them. York is a busy place. You came, and took the pig keeper's house, and for a time all seemed to go well. You kept to your work and we kept to ours, and though we did not come upon one another often, it was good to see smoke coming again from the hut. My sister especially liked having you near. You would go to the river together sometimes of an evening, and you would tell her all that you had seen on your travels."

"And the rest of you?"

There were stirrings in the yard beyond the shed, the sound of an ax chopping wood. Nat slowly got to his feet, favoring the injured leg.

"I have no grudge against you, Daniel. But it would be better if you didn't stay. Once you are well, I mean. . . ." He stopped, peering around the doorway into the yard, then lowered his voice: "My father once had his fortune told him by an old woman—a descendant of the Druids, she claimed. It said that a young buck would come into his life and change it for either ill or good. Since then, he has waited for this young stranger with a curious sort of welcome. And when you were among the first to fall ill—and worse yet, in his eyes, the only one to recover—both he and

Jasper, my brother, fear that the evil may have been brought to York in your body; while you will live to travel on, you will leave death behind for the rest of us. If I were you, truly, I would leave here as soon as you are able. I tell you this as a friend."

THE NOISE of the chopping continued on into the evening—a rhythmical, labored sound, as though the woodcutter breathed rage into every stroke, venting his silent fury upon the oak and pine before him. Now and then the ax missed its mark, making a dull, scraping sound, not the clean sharp crack of wood being split. Then Dan would hear an oath from the lips of Ambrose Faw, followed sometimes by a long, weary, "Ahhhhh." Occasionally Jasper would pass by the door of the shed, but he did not come in and he did not speak.

Why, Dan wondered, when life was so full of natural calamities, did men have to make more of their own choosing? When he might be of use to them, might even help save their lives, why this intrusion of distrust, this wall between them?

He could believe that what Nat said was true, that he was unwelcome here, but not to Orlenda. Dan had not come all this way to find her, only to leave her now. He remembered the fear on her face that afternoon at the river when she told him about the pestilence. If the family would not go with him, if he could not persuade them to leave, then he would take Orlenda alone.

He was conscious of silence outside, of the end to

the chopping. And suddenly there was a rolling, clunking noise. The ax landed with a thud against the wall of the shed where Dan was lying. Then all was still.

5

HE WAS A PRISONER, not of Ambrose Faw, but of his own body. Dan could take no action until his legs regained their strength, make no plans until his head cleared. He could no more will himself strong and able than he could force the family's trust.

He slowly turned over on his stomach and attempted a push-up there on the straw. He could raise himself only a few inches, then fell flat on his face. Tears of helplessness came to his eyes, and he rolled over on his back, letting them come, surprised and grateful at the strange relief they brought. He was like a young babe, born into this century by a mere whim of fate, dependent upon the very girl he had come to save. He could not even walk without leaning on Orlenda. His coming here was a joke.

Hadn't life always been so, however? Weren't both birth and death mere accidents, completely overlooked by the stars? When you examined the course of history, of wars fought and children slain, was there any reason to live constructively, any reward for being noble? If life was a joke, then men were clowns, and living for oneself—for the moment —was the only rational thing to do.

And yet . . .

He remembered her face there by the river: *I have been born into the worst of all possible times, truly I have,* she had told him. Ever since he had faced the possibility of a hereditary disease robbing him of his own future, he had wanted Orlenda to live—had been obsessed with it. And strangely, he had felt somehow more alive—even now, sick as he'd been— than he'd felt before. Every minute seemed precious.

Because of Orlenda, he knew what it meant to be needed; and in feeling needed, he had found a purpose. What strength he had would be hers. What determination and patience and foresight, that he would give her also. If nothing else, however—if all the rest failed him—he wanted to give her hope.

His resolve thus strengthened, he let the shadows engulf him, the straw enfold him, and he gave himself to sleep.

Dreams rolled in, one on top of another—blending, separating, and coming together again. He tumbled over and over himself in time, from Asia to Europe, from India to France. He was a Roman, an Iberian, a Celt, a Brigante. . . . He was lying in wait for the gypsies who would arrive in Britain several hundred years hence, mingling their blood with the farmers and herdsmen who were already here, then he flowed on again, through oceans to rivers to ponds to streams, adrift with the dreams of all the ancestors before him, alive with the hopes of all who would come after.

There was a squeaking and scratching so close to his ear that, thinking of mosquitoes, Dan raised one hand and gave a swat. His palm hit something warm and furry, and the shed was rent with a high-pitched squeal.

He rose up swiftly on one elbow, staring about him in the early morning light. Only a few feet away, something stared back at him with small, unblinking eyes, and then he saw more of them: rats.

Dan sprang to his feet, backing out the door of the shed, feeling his arms for bites. He edged over to the stump in the yard and sat down, huddled there in his tunic, shivering in the misty dawn that spread out now in the sky above York.

Why hadn't he remembered? Why hadn't he told them? Rats were spreading the plague all over Europe, and no one seemed to know. He had been half delirious when Orlenda found him by the river, and it had not occurred to him till now. He thought suddenly of banging on the door of Ambrose's cottage, of waking all the people in the surrounding homes, of telling them all to plug up the ratholes, clean up the filth, burn the rubbish, yet even as he thought it, he knew how ridiculous it would sound to them.

"There have always been rats," they would say.

He watched the sky turn from deep gray to silver and at last to pink. He could just make out the shape of the village in which he was staying, a small group of cottages beyond the western walls of York. There was Bootham Bar, the huge gateway, looming up against the sky, its spiked portcullis closed against intruders, and somewhere the night watch roamed about, waiting to be relieved. Behind him, on down the hill, was the Ouse.

He thought of it again—the river. No wall could keep it out, no pestilence stop its flow, no army check its current. It had been there before Agricola began his conquest of Britain and had been there still when the Romans had gone. It had been used by invaders to conquer the city and had carried their butchered bodies, at their defeat, back to the Humber and out to the sea. The river was there when Dan and his parents had visited York in another age, another time, and would be there still, no matter what calamities befell England. There was peace in knowing it would always remain among the rushes.

The door to the cottage opened, and Orlenda came out. She was pulling straw from her hair and brushing it from her clothes. When she saw Dan sitting on the stump, she came over.

"You're up so early, Daniel?"

"I'm feeling better," he told her, realizing, in fact, that he had actually walked to the stump himself without help and had the strength now to sit up. His head felt clearer, his muscles less sore.

Orlenda bent down and hugged him tightly. "It's so *good* to see you better," she said. "You'll stay here with us now, won't you?"

He reached up and gently stroked her hair, glad that she did not move away from him. "None of us should stay, Orlenda. I want to go away and take you with me, someplace where there's no sickness."

"We've talked about leaving, Daniel, but where would we go? Who is there that would take us in?"

"Listen." He turned suddenly and clutched her arm so forcefully that she startled. "I know what causes the pestilence. I remember. It's the rat."

"The rat?" She looked at him incredulously. "Daniel, how could you know that? Not even the wisest men of York have said so."

"It's true, Orlenda. Rats are spreading the disease."

She continued staring and then broke into laughter. Her voice had a harsh sound that grated on his ears. "Rats have always been with us," she said. "You might as well try to get rid of the common fly."

IN THE DAYS TO COME, Dan bided his time, waiting for his body to heal and the trust between him and the Faws to mend. Each morning found him stronger, so that when evening came, he had accomplished a bit more for the family. Each time he looked at Ambrose, however, and Jasper, the older brother, Dan found no warmth in their eyes at all.

When the day's work was over, Orlenda would

come to him and sit, encouraging him to eat a bit more—to walk with her up to the road or down to the river, pushing his endurance a little further. When his strength was spent, she would let him rest. Then she and Rachel would sit nearby, weaving garlands of daisies and dandelions, which Rachel would drape around her and parade about the yard, making Dan laugh.

He kept his distance from Ambrose, and Ambrose from him. When Orlenda's father left of a morning to work his field, Dan tried his hand at woodchopping, and each day he stacked a bit more wood for their fire. He drew the water, fed the pigs, raked the yard, and when there were no other jobs at hand, he set about plugging up the ratholes. Rose and the granny watched him with laughing eyes, but they humored him and let him be, for he told stories to Rachel as he worked and kept her amused.

On the path to the river, people sometimes reached out to Dan and touched him, then crossed themselves, as though whatever charm had made him well might rub off on them, should they need it. But there were others who gave him dark looks and whispered among themselves, and Jasper was one of them.

Orlenda's older brother went to work each day for a lutemaker inside the walls of York. He took his breakfast in the morning sitting off on the far side of the clearing, then left when the sun came over the roof of the house. He had said nothing, voiced no welcome, since Dan had come to live in the shed, and Dan tried to do nothing that might provoke him, knowing how tenuous was his own stay as a guest.

Orlenda helped her father in the fields, carrying hay on her strong back or driving the ox ahead of the plow. Nat, with his stiff leg, hobbled after her and did what he could, but would return home early in the day and stretch out on the grass to rest.

On the fifth day, Dan ventured over to the neighboring hut, that of Old William, who, having become slightly deaf and arthritic, had turned his fields over to the Faws. He spent his hours puttering about the yard—tending his geese, feeding his lambs, and watching for the first cherries of the season.

"Good morning," Dan said, coming up beside the man who sat on a bench beneath his cherry tree. Old William wore a curious number of pouches on strings about his body, like a peddler of purses, and his feet were bare, calloused around the edges with age and country living.

The man turned and stared at him hard for a moment, then, recognizing who he was, began to grin, opening the dark toothless cavern of his mouth. He patted the bench for Dan to sit down, for they had not actually talked together that Dan could remember. Dan was glad that his reception was so friendly, but within a short time he began to wonder.

"Up and about, up and about," Old William said. "Today you are here, tomorrow there, next week you will be in Chester, eh?"

Dan smiled. "I'm feeling much better."

Old William merrily poked at him with his walking stick. "And what's the secret, Daniel the Young, the Scribe? What do you carry in your belt that saves your skin?"

"It's mere luck, Old William. I carry nothing." Dan could tell at once that the neighbor did not believe him.

"Nothing? Nothing, you say?" The man's nostrils seemed to spread, and the sagging flesh beneath his jaw began to tighten. "It is only luck, you think, that spares one man and takes another?"

For a moment Dan considered telling him about the rats, but he knew he might as well save his breath. As it turned out, Old William did not wait for an answer. His face relaxed once more, his eyes began to smile, and suddenly he began to laugh:

"A fig on the doctors, that's what I say, and I'm still here to say it, so that's something! If it's song that's wanted, one calls for a musician, eh? If it's cake that's needed, one goes to the baker. But if there's evil afoot and magic is wanted, one goes to the magician."

He thrust one hand deep inside the pouch that hung on his left side and pulled out something small and honey-colored.

"A hazelnut," he said, holding it up between a dirty thumbnail and a forefinger for Dan's inspection. "To defend against the power of witchcraft."

Then he squirreled it away once more and dug into the pouch on his right.

"A gallstone," he said, "from an old ewe." He paused. "Yes, I think it was a ewe. Or was it a goat, now? A she-goat?" He stared off in the distance, trying to remember, then shook his head. "Well, no matter." Back went the gallstone, and this time he pulled a piece of paper from the pouch that was slung over his shoulder. He held it out at arm's length so he could see it, but because he could not read, he finally passed it on to Dan, keeping hold of the edge so that he would not lose possession.

Dan leaned forward and studied it. At first, it appeared to be a meaningless design of letters, but then he saw that it was the word Abracadabra, repeated line after line, growing shorter each time as the final letter was removed:

```
          A B R A C A D A B R A
           A B R A C A D A B R
            A B R A C A D A B
             A B R A C A D A
              A B R A C A D
               A B R A C A
                A B R A C
                 A B R A
                  A B R
                   A B
                    A
```

"You got this from the magician, also?" Dan asked.

Old William nodded gravely. " 'Twas a Roman

brought it here to Britain, he said as a cure against the fever." He lowered his voice to a whisper. "But in truth, it protects against the evil eye."

The man is mad, thought Dan.

There was one more pouch to be got into, and before Old William opened the one about his neck, he made the sign of a cross, moving his lips as he did so. Then he took out a handful of small slips of paper, each with writing on it, returning them all to the pouch again except one. There was writing on it, Dan could see, but before he had a chance to read it, Old William picked it up between thumb and forefinger and popped it in his mouth, swallowing twice to get it down. Dan stared.

Old William seemed to know what he was thinking, for he said, "It's fool's play, you know. The Church passes them around—prayers they are—to be swallowed once a day. I will die of a stomach full of paper, and then they will say, 'See? The pestilence did not touch him!'" He laughed aloud at his own joke, then grew suddenly serious again. "I'll try them all—the magician, the doctor, the priest, the peddler. If you wear one charm, why not wear them all?"

He turned his red-veined eyes to Dan again. "It's all luck, you say? Then may she smile on me. Old William would like to go some other way than to die in the street, dragged off by the dogs."

"It's a scary business," Dan agreed. "Have you ever thought of leaving—of getting away from York while the pestilence is raging?"

"Like one of the rats, eh? Abandoning ship?" The old man turned toward the road. "Every day now, they go by—people, carts, fine ladies on horse-back. . . . 'Where are they all going?' I say to myself. When they get there, it will be as crowded as it is here! No, Old William will stay put. Someone's got to feed the lambs, tend the geese. . . ."

"It's hard to know what to do," Dan said. "Where are there horses to be had, do you know?"

The old man looked at him curiously. "You wouldn't be afraid the pestilence would strike you twice, would you?"

"No, I'm thinking of the Faws."

"Ah, then." He shook his head. "Just this morn-ing a woman came by asking if I'd a horse to spare. They've all been taken, I'm afraid. People even go afoot with packs on their backs, loaded down like mules." He shook his head. "They will be dead by the time they reach the crossroads, as surely as if the pestilence had found them first. Wait a week, till the owners are dead, and then there will be horses to spare."

A deep despair welled up in Dan's chest, and he knew he must not stay here talking to this man any longer. The ox—Ambrose's ox—was the only an-swer, laden down with food and bedding; but the journey would be slow. How would the grandmother travel? Thoughts spun wildly through his head. They could rig up her chair, perhaps; put it on poles. The rest would walk. There was Rachel, of course, and she would tire, so someone would carry her. . . . It seemed less and less a good idea, but then he thought of Orlenda, young and spirited, and resolved once more to find a way to take her out of York.

Old William grabbed at his sleeve as he stood up and drew him closer. His eyes were crinkled once again and his dark mouth opened in silent laughter.

"I'll tell you the secret!" he said. "Dancing! Jesting! Merriment and singing! That's why the pestilence goes around me and lets me be. Gloominess is fatal. If I have no one to joke with, I sit under my tree and smile to myself."

Perhaps not so mad after all, Dan thought as he made his way back through the orchard. Whatever life was left for him, Old William would not waste a minute. That night, he decided, he would lay his plan before the Faws. He would suggest that they go north, where the plague had not yet been, and that they leave as soon as they were able. He would check over their sandals when he got back to the hut, mend any straps that were broken, see about a chair for the grandmother and some baskets to carry their clothes.

There was a strap missing on Rachel's sandal, and Dan sat down on the stump in the clearing to mend it. Nat was returning home from the field, and he stretched out on the ground beside him, rubbing one shoulder, his hands grimy from the handles of the plow.

"Uhhh," he groaned softly to himself. He left off

rubbing his shoulder and rubbed his leg instead. "The leg is worse today, I don't know why."

Dan handed him a dipper of water from the drinking bucket and went on with his work. "How did you come to be a soldier in France?" he asked finally.

Nat drank, then lay back again and stared up at the sky. "It was the child in me," he said at last. "I looked at a soldier's longbow and wanted to use it. I wanted adventure—a chance to see the land across the channel. I'd heard of a knight going to war—the lord of a manor, he was. So I hired myself out. I was to ride a horse beside the master and do for him in battle."

He put his hands under his head and lay very still. "England won, and the knight came back a hero. Even his horse was decorated. He entered Micklegate Bar to a blare of trumpets, and I walked behind in the dung. A song was composed for him about his bravery in the Battle of Crécy. He had not even a scratch, while both I and my horse were injured. My horse, in fact, was dead. During the celebration that followed in the manor, I slipped away and came home."

He gave a prolonged sigh and glanced toward the house. The words came now like small explosions from his throat, and he winced as though their very utterance hurt his chest: "I neither told my family that I was leaving nor that I was coming back again. They heard the news each time from people in the city. And when they gathered about to hear all that had happened in France, I had nothing to tell them except stories of horses screaming, their sides split open, and men left rotting on the field."

"Nat," Dan said suddenly, feeling that now was the time to say it, that Nat would understand. "I want to take Orlenda away from here to someplace where it's safe. I want her to have a chance at life."

Nat looked at him curiously. "Where would you go? My father once talked of Scotland should the pestilence come to York, for his people are from there. But Scotland is a long way off, and there are robbers on the roads. At least here we have a house, a bed. . . ."

"We would have to start out and see," Dan told him. "Surely there's someplace that has not been touched by disease. If we go, will you come with us?"

If Nat agreed to go, perhaps they would all come too. Only then could Dan be certain that Orlenda would leave.

"I can't travel very fast on this leg of mine."

"I know. If only we had horses. But there are new cases of sickness springing up every day, Nat. I hear them whispered about at the river, out on the road. . . . This morning two women were talking. The butcher, they say, fell ill, and his wife and daughter along with him. His shop is closed."

"The butcher!" Nat exclaimed.

Suddenly the air was split with a scream from inside the house. Rachel ran out, her face white, her eyes huge, but it was not she who had screamed. And then Rose appeared in the doorway like a wild woman, running down the path to where Dan and Nat were sitting.

"It's the granny!" she said.

THE OLD WOMAN was sitting on a bench by the hearth, her head down, arms hanging loosely at her sides. Rose hung back at the doorway, clutching Rachel to her, and the small girl stood motionless, her face buried in her mother's skirt.

"Granny?" Dan knelt down beside the woman.

The head moved and the old lady lifted her head, her eyes clouding over. As she did so, she was seized suddenly with a violent coughing fit. As she drew her hand away from her mouth, her palm was spotted with blood.

Dan went to Rose and Nat, who had now reached the doorway. "Don't touch her," he instructed gently. "You musn't go near her, any of you."

He went out to the low barn where Ambrose kept the ox and took more straw. Spreading it over the floor of the shed, which had been his room, he covered it next with Granny's own blanket and then, picking the small woman up in his arms, surprised at the lightness of her frail body, carried her to the bed he had made for her and put her down. Against the sound of Rose's crying, he took cold water and sat beside the old woman, bathing her face. Her cheeks were so hot to the touch that he wondered the heat alone did not kill her.

When she slept finally, he went back out and washed his hands with lye soap.

"Yesterday she was fine," Rose sobbed. "She stood out on the road with the butcher's wife, chattering like a magpie. This morning she seemed merely tired, and I thought nothing of it. And then the coughing began, and I noticed the blood. . . ."

"A doctor should be called at once," Dan said.

"Perhaps he can give her a draught," Rose said desperately. "You go, Daniel, will you? The scholars in York speak French, you know, and if he spoke it to me, I'd not know a word he was saying."

"You'll find him in a house at the end of Goodramgate Street," Nat told him. "Tell him who you are —Daniel the Scribe, the one who recovered."

Dan had no delusions as he set out along the dirt road, through the sycamore and sweet chestnut trees, that the doctor could save the old granny. It was not for that purpose that he had suggested calling one, but rather to protect Orlenda and the others from the illness that was all about them now.

Bootham Bar was open, the drawbridge down, and Dan entered, trying to orient himself by the York of the 1980s that he remembered. The other great gates of the city were situated about the walls like the points of a compass: Monk Bar to the north, Walmgate Bar to the east, and Micklegate Bar to the south, the gateway through which kings entered York in stately procession. The cathedral was to his left, and beyond that, he knew, Goodramgate. That much would not have changed.

He was unprepared for the smells, however. Since he had awakened from the stupor of his illness, his nose had been assaulted with odors so numerous and pungent that they frequently affected his stomach. Now, in the heart of the city itself, it seemed as though the high walls trapped the odors that might have dissipated over the countryside, and he felt immersed in the stench of fish, of unwashed bodies, and animal dung. As he reached the end of Petergate Street, he smelled the rancid odor of meat from the Shambles; and after he turned off onto Goodramgate, he was sickened with the noxious odors of a bell foundry.

Hanging from various shops were huge signs advertising the craft or profession of the owner—a large hand for a glovemaker, a boot for a cobbler, a tooth for the extractor. . . . The barking of dogs added to the din of the street hawkers selling strawberries and cheeses and hot meats. On one corner, Dan stopped as a funeral procession came wending down a narrow lane. A priest walked ahead holding a cross, and the bier on which the coffin rested was followed by a tearful group of mourners. For a few minutes, until the procession had passed, the street hawkers fell silent, and the crowds drew back. Then the dogs, which had slunk off into doorways at the sight of the black-robed priest, came out again and followed the end of the entourage, howling. Finally the strawberry hawker picked up her cry once more, and before the last of the mourners had disappeared, the street had grown as noisy as before.

The doctor's home was near Monk Bar. It was a wooden two-story house of dark brown with over-hanging windows above. A sign on one corner said simply, "Physician." Dan went up to the door and knocked.

There did not appear to be anyone at home, for no one came and nobody called out. He pounded again, and this time he caught a glimpse of a woman peeking at him from an upper window. She ducked quickly when she saw him looking at her, but it was too late.

"Hello?" Dan called up. "Is the doctor in?"

Inch by inch, the woman's head emerged, and finally her face came into view for just an instant.

"He's not at home," she called down. "He's out with the sick, and I'm not so good myself."

Somehow Dan did not believe her.

"I'm Daniel the Scribe—the one who recovered —and I've need of a draught for an old woman."

The head came out all the way this time, and the woman studied him carefully.

"Bless me, it *is* you, and walking, too! Just a min-ute, lad, and I'll open the door."

He waited and heard her steps approaching from inside. The stout, red-haired woman opened the door a crack, peeked out at the street, then opened it wider and drew him in quickly.

"I never know what's waiting for me at the door when I open it these days," she said guiltily. "It's a sin, I know, to shut out the sick, but if the pestilence strikes the doctor, who's to care for his patients?" She crossed the room to a smaller one in back, Dan following.

"Yesterday I heard a banging and opened the door to find a babe thrust out at me, blood oozing from its mouth, the mother shrieking at me to take it in. Was all I could do to keep it out of my arms and get me the door bolted again, and I says to my husband, 'We'll both be dead before evening if I open the door again,' so I've shut it for good. He goes about and asks questions now of a house before he enters, and if it's the pestilence, he commits them to the Lord's care and goes on to the next."

She stopped abruptly and turned to Dan. "Well, now. Let's have a look at you. A miracle, that's what you are. Stick out your tongue."

Dan did as he was told, and she examined his throat and then the backs of his hands.

"A little thin, you are, but you are healed as surely as this house is standing. And what did you take for it? Tell me."

"I remember almost nothing. I was given some gruel, that's all."

"You drank no draughts? Applied no plasters?"
"No."

"No doctor lanced your boils or bled you?"

"No. I only slept."

"Ahhh. Truly a miracle." She looked at him for a long time, then said suddenly. "Sit down now. I've scarcely a soul to talk to but the doctor, and he's never in. God favors you, He does. But not all would think so." She shook her head gravely. "You've heard the reports—about the Jews?"

Dan had no idea what she was talking about and did not want to get into a long conversation. He was anxious to get back before Orlenda came in from the fields. But he dared not hurry her. "No, I haven't heard. . . ."

"When people feel helpless," the woman said, "they often look for something they can control—a target for their anger. And in many of the cities on the Continent, where the pestilence is raging, they have chosen the Jews."

"They blame the Jews? Why?"

"They accuse them of poisoning the wells—Jews and lepers too, poor things."

"But aren't Jews dying of the disease also?"

"Of course. But because the Jews prefer drinking water from running streams and Christians use the wells, it has been rumored that the Jews are poisoning the wells. In Basle all the Jews were penned up in wooden buildings and burned alive. They were burned at Stuttgart, and then in Lindau. In Speyer the bodies of the murdered were piled in great wine casks and sent floating down the Rhine. Then the persecutions spread to Dresden and Strasbourg and Mainz. Every day, it seems, the doctor hears more news from abroad. In Hausa, Jews were walled up alive in their houses; and in other places they themselves set their homes on fire and perish before the mobs can get at them. Why, do you suppose, when nature turns against mankind, mankind turns against itself? Not even the Pope, who has condemned the persecution, can stop it."

"The world has gone mad," Dan said, sickened by the stories, feeling an even greater desire to take Orlenda away.

"Quite mad. And yet here and there is a small voice of reason. In Cologne, we have heard, the magistrates declared the pestilence to be a scourge of God and will not permit the persecution of Jews in their town. But people everywhere are frightened. And when they are frightened enough, they panic. They want to find a reason, a cause." Her green eyes focused on Dan again. "There will be those who wish you ill, Daniel, just because you have recovered, just because there is no one else to blame. You must watch yourself." She put her hands in her lap. "And now, what did you come here for? I babble on and on—a brook, that's what I am. A draught for an old woman, you said?"

"I was sent by Rose Faw, wife of Ambrose. The old granny's taken sick. It's the pestilence, and I'm afraid for the others."

The doctor's wife crossed herself. "Has she boils?"

"I don't know. She has a fever."

"And does she cough? Does it come up blood?"

"She was coughing blood not an hour ago."

The doctor's wife shook her head. "She'll not last more than two days if that, poor soul."

"Is there anything we can do for the others?" Dan pleaded. "There are children in the family."

"Of course there are children. There are always children, and death finds them out as surely as the old ones with little life left in them. The children and the old ones—they always go first."

"I've put her in a shed outside, away from the others."

"Good. That's good. No one must touch her except you, and it's only a miracle saved you."

"What medicine do you have as a precaution for the others?"

"The Lord only knows what to give! But a little theriac might help. I'll ladle some out for you."

"I've only a shilling."

"Well, a shilling's worth, then. It's not a cheap draught, you know. Sixty ingredients, that's what it takes, and ten years to age. But I'll give you some extra anyway."

She took the top off a large crock in one corner, revealing a dark liquid with a dank odor. Carefully she began ladling it out into a jar.

"What does the doctor think is the cause of this pestilence?" Dan asked her.

"If he knew, we'd have us a fine house in London now, wouldn't we! Be invited to meet the King! Last year, when the sickness was raging on the Continent, the doctor got a pronouncement from the University of Paris. It was the planets, they said, responsible for the pestilence. And they went on to pronounce that in the Great Sea near India, the waters had boiled and heaved until a stinking mist crept over the land. Reptiles and frogs were bred from the corruption, they said, and spread the disease. Well, that might be true for India, but where are there so many reptiles and frogs hereabouts, I'd like to know?"

"It's the rats," Dan told her.

"Eh?"

"The rats. I'm sure of it."

"Well, everybody has an opinion," she said, and came back over to him with a jar in her hands. "I'll tell you what my husband thinks: it's the breath, that's what it is. Mothers breathe it on their babes, the babes on their grannies, the grannies on the peddler, the peddler on the boys. . . . No doubt but that it's worse in the cities, and York is the dirtiest city in the Kingdom, if that has anything to do with it."

She gave him the theriac and walked him to the door. "Some say it's in the clouds, and the wind blows it about from place to place, skipping a town here, settling down on another one there. Some say it's Christ's arrows, and that only the Virgin Mother can intervene and save us. They tell me the Pope was spared by spending summer last between two big fires kept burning day and night. But what would happen if we all sat between fires here in York, eh? Burn the whole town, that's what."

She put one hand on the door and then said, "Touch me, lad. I know it's a priest should give blessing, but the Lord chose you to favor, and there's no harm in it that I can see. If there's a charm about you, maybe it will pass on to me."

Somewhat embarrassed, Dan touched her on the forehead, and thus comforted, she opened the door and let him out.

"Don't waste the theriac on the granny," she told him. "Some each day for the others, that's what the doctor recommends. Tell them to sprinkle their nostrils with rosewater and vinegar and pray God spare us. That's all there is to do."

DAN HAD ALMOST reached the path to the cottage when a strong arm seized him about his neck from behind, cutting off his breath. His hands were pinned to his body, and it was all he could do to keep hold of the jar of theriac.

Robbers. He could scarcely believe that they would attack him here, in the middle of the village and within sight of the walls of York. Were they so desperate for medicine? He began to struggle, more to breathe than to free himself, and the next moment found himself released and spun about. He was face to face with Jasper.

He backed off, staring at him, rubbing his neck.

"Why did you come here?" Jasper muttered. "Why did you bring this thing upon us?"

"You can't believe that," Dan said incredulously.

"It's you who fell ill with it—you who carries the evilness about in your body."

"I know nothing more than you, Jasper. I don't know why I recovered, unless it was Orlenda's good care of me. Surely that's not reason enough to hate me."

"The butcher is dead," Jasper said grimly. "It was the first news I heard in York this morning. And when I reached the shop, the lutemaker had fallen ill. Now, my grandmother. All around me, friends are dying, and it was not so until you came."

"Have I been to Germany, then, and France?" Dan retorted, somewhat angrily. "Did I start the pestilence in Italy?"

"I don't know where you are from," Jasper answered, "but you have cheated death, and only a demon from Hell can do that. If you stay in York, you will die of something else, if not by me, then by others. That I can promise you."

Jasper moved away then, his eyes glowering like those of a forest animal, and he disappeared among the trees.

6

THE FOLLOWING DAY, the granny died. All night long she had lain with swollen tongue protruding from cracked, dry lips, trying to drink the water that Dan held to her mouth. It was Dan who witnessed her final breath, and Jasper, whose narrowed eyes followed him when he left the shed. The pestilence had taken not only the old woman's life but her dignity as well. Her frail arms and legs had become spotted with blotches of black, and everything about her—her breath, her spittle, her urine—gave off an unbearable stench. The fetid smell issuing from the shed where she lay was so overpowering that not even the pigs, rooting about in the yard, would go near.

Ambrose sat on the doorstep of his house, his jaw tense, eyes staring off into the trees. The word had gone out that the old woman was dead, and the gravediggers would be there before nightfall.

"It's a sorry lot they are, too," he commented to

the others who stood or sat about the yard in what would be their last vigil. "Galley slaves, convicts—men who've got their freedom in return for dragging off bodies. Vultures, they are, robbing the pockets of the dead before putting them under."

"We should be burying her ourselves," Nat said grimly.

"It's against the ordinance," Rose reminded.

"I'd as soon dig a hole myself back of the barn and put her in it," Nat went on. "She'll not have the grave she wanted."

Dan sat silently next to Rachel, who leaned against him, clutching her rag doll. There was a tension in the air so thick he could almost stretch out his hand and touch it. No one had slept the night before, and tempers flared, alternating with exhaustion and grief. But it was fear that permeated their talk—fear and a deep melancholia of hopelessness.

"The men that dig the graves are the same ones sent to carry the sick off to the plague-houses, that's what I heard," Ambrose said. "They've got one hand on the sick and the other on the shovel."

"What will we do when the cemeteries are full?" Nat wondered aloud. "In France, in Avignon, they say, they buried them in a field, and when that was full, the river Rhône was consecrated and the bodies tipped into it. Sometimes they washed up on the bank further on, and pestilence broke out there."

"It's a peril sent to wipe out all mankind," Rose moaned, her eyes dull. "On the Continent, I've heard, black flags fly from towers in villages where the pestilence is greatest; buildings have been left unfinished, fields unplowed. Dikes have crumbled and salt water seeps back in to sour the lowlands. The work of centuries has been destroyed, and there are few people left to set things right again. The world will never be the same." She sighed deeply. "I never thought I would know the way I would die. It will take us all, one by one, and the last to go will have no one to mourn him."

"Stop it!" Orlenda sprang forward suddenly, her hands over her ears, her face contorted. She dropped to her knees, sobbing loudly, her shoulders shaking. "We're animals, all of us! Not a one of us touched Granny except Daniel, or kissed her even. We've let her die alone, and now we sit talking of unspeakable things. We just stay here and let it happen!"

Dan wanted to go to her at once, to hold her, to promise he'd take her away, but he dared not do it yet. Rose watched her daughter sadly but seemed to have no energy left to comfort her, and Orlenda buried her head in her lap, crying bitterly.

Ambrose was unnerved by her tears. "Do you think we're the only ones to suffer, Orlenda?" he asked helplessly. "Everyone lives under the threat of pestilence. Everyone is frightened."

"That doesn't help!" Orlenda said angrily. "If any of you were to die, do you think I would feel better knowing that the butcher died also? If I fall ill myself, will it comfort you to know that I'll join the butcher's daughter? I want to *live!* I want us *all* to live! I want Rachel to have a chance at something. If horrible things are going to happen, let's get away from here while there's time. Can't we even try?"

There were tears in Ambrose's eyes as well. Dan could see them glistening there at the corners. Even on Ambrose, they did not seem out of place.

"Daughter," he answered, "don't you think that if I knew of a town that was safe, I would have taken you there already? Don't you think that if there was a land where we could all live protected, we would leave this very night? People flee to the woods and when the food is gone, they come back again. Why give up a house when we might fall ill in a stranger's barn? Why give up our beds when the pestilence may overtake us on the road? No one knows where it will—" He stopped talking suddenly, his words seemingly stuck in his throat, and jerked his head toward the low branch of a tree. "Look."

Heads turned and Dan looked to where he was nodding. There sat four magpies, three together on the right, and a little further on, the fourth.

Without taking her eyes from the tree, Rose intoned, "One is for bad luck, two are for good, three for a wedding, four for a death. . . ."

"Perhaps it's a death that's come already," Nat said quickly. "Perhaps it means the Granny."

"It is like the end of the world," Ambrose said, despair in his eyes. "Did I bring my sons and daughters into the world to be carried away on a cart? Did

I bring them into the world to lie rotting in the street, their clothes torn off by the dogs? Did I bring them into the world so that they would see death all about them, and I would be robbed of grandchildren?"

A huge sigh escaped his lips, and he went on as though talking to himself: "When the children were little, Rose and I said they would see a better world than we; York would be more prosperous, our cottage would be theirs, and perhaps we would even leave them an ox or two—a cow, perhaps—and a few pigs and sheep as well. More than we had to start with, the Lord knows. And now . . . God forgive me that I brought them into the world at all."

"Ambrose," Dan said quietly, "I would like to help in any way that I can. Perhaps Orlenda is right, you should leave York while there is still a chance you will escape the pestilence. Between us, we could pack our things this very night and be on the road by morning. We could load up the ox and leave the sheep and pigs to Old William. If Rachel tired, we could take turns carrying her. We would trust to the goodness of others to give us meat and milk along the way, and perhaps I could earn a sixpence for us now and then by writing a letter. I beg you to consider it."

The silence that followed was awful, for it was as though everyone had stopped breathing. Orlenda's sobs seemed to have stopped in mid-breath, and all eyes were upon him. Dan could not tell from their expressions what they were thinking. He desperately searched their faces for some sign that they understood his offer, that he had not upset them.

Finally Ambrose said, "You are a guest among us, a stranger. You press your luck."

"I meant no offense, Ambrose. Truly."

Dan wanted the conversation to continue. He wanted to draw them out, but at that moment they heard a cart stopping on the road above, and all turned to watch as three men came down the path toward the house carrying a wood coffin. Rose began to wail softly, and Ambrose stood up to meet them.

"You've a body here?" the man in front was asking. His ruddy face had the look of a man who had just come from the ale house, and his tunic was pulled up at the hem and tucked in his belt, revealing his long dirty stockings.

Ambrose surveyed him with contempt. "We have a woman. An old woman in need of a gentle burial."

"It's all the same to the dead," the man answered, weaving slightly.

His two companions, their eyes dull, hung back.

"But it's not the same to me," Ambrose told him. "I want her taken gently." He nodded toward the shed. "In there. Wrap her well in her blanket and bury it too. It's all that goes with her, save our prayers."

The first gravedigger approached the shed and when he was a few feet from it, turned his head abruptly and uttered an oath. Then, pulling up a scarf about his neck until it covered his nose, he went inside and emerged a moment later dragging the old woman by the heels.

Jasper leaped to his feet. "Use the blanket, you swine!" he roared.

One of the men went back into the shed, returning with the blanket, and they rolled the grandmother onto one end of it and continued rolling until she was encased in her last possession. Then, stuffing her into the coffin, they put on the lid, hoisted it to their shoulders, and started up the path for the cart.

Halfway there, however, one of the men stumbled and fell. The coffin tipped backwards, one end striking the ground. The lid came off, and the grandmother fell halfway out, as though bowing to the very men who took her away.

Jasper rushed forward, the veins standing out on his neck, his eyes huge. He picked up a stick and went after the men, a strange cry in his throat. He began striking at them about the shoulders, and they, in turn, swung back groggily. It was only when Ambrose and Nat intervened that the coffin was dumped unceremoniously on the cart and the oxen goaded into moving on up the road.

Slowly Jasper came back to the clearing and sat exhausted on the stump, head down, shoulders heaving. When he lifted his eyes at last, they rested on Dan, and he sat that way, never moving.

A RAIN FELL THAT NIGHT, and Dan sought another shelter besides the place he had been sleeping under a tree. He retreated at last to the low barn where Ambrose kept his animals and found a spot for himself on the hay near the roof. The ox and the sheep and pigs were kept behind a rail on the opposite side; the ox gave a strange sort of snort as Dan entered, as though warning against intrusion.

Dan was exhausted from his vigil of the night before, but more so from his effort to discuss their leaving. It had been the wrong time to suggest it, he concluded. The family was tired, their nerves strained; they were in no condition to discuss such a move, much less to pack up before morning. Dan was almost too tired to care. He made no plans, dreamed no dreams, but gave himself over to sleep. Once he awakened to hear the ox lowing again, but then his eyes rolled back and he reveled in his unconsciousness.

Perhaps it was because he had slept so soundly, refreshing himself so thoroughly, that a slight sound toward dawn awoke him at last. It was a mere creaking, like the noise of an open door blowing slightly in the wind.

He opened his eyes and lay without moving, wondering whether it was light already beyond the roof. It was warm at the top of the hay next to the rafters, and he decided that perhaps it was this that had wakened him. Noiselessly he rolled down into an open space by the wall where the air coming in through the slats was cooler. He lay listening to the soft crunch of hay in the ox's mouth, and then realized it was not the sound of chewing at all, but of footsteps.

He sat up on one elbow, but could not see over the hay behind which he was lying. Something kept him from rising up, from giving himself away. If it was Orlenda looking for him, she would have called his name. If it was Old William, his plodding footsteps would have sounded on the earthen floor, and he would be talking to the ox in his low, gentle voice, or chasing out the pigs and sending them to forage in the morning mist.

These footsteps, however, went a few paces and stopped. Dan lay motionless there on his side, his heart pounding fiercely, his breath coming fast, and he opened his mouth to let it escape noiselessly.

There was a light then in the barn. A candle had been lit. Through the sparse hay at one end, Dan could just make out a shoulder, an arm, the calf of a leg, and there, at the side, an ax. He knew at once it was Jasper.

And then there was Ambrose's voice, low and mumbling, from somewhere just inside the doorway.

"Ahhhh," Dan heard him say. And, after a pause, "Then do what needs to be done."

There were footsteps again, receding. Dan saw the leg move, and next the arm. The ox lowed again, and then there was the sound of the animal being led away, and the light from the candle dimmed, along with Jasper's footsteps.

Dan sat up, wondering. Were they leaving? Was

the family moving on without him, hoping they'd be gone before he had awakened?

He rose up and jumped down onto the floor, frightening the four sheep, which stampeded across the sleeping pigs and huddled, bleating, in the far corner. Dan went outside.

Jasper was leading the ox down to the river. The door to the house was closed, the windows dark. No candles burned that he could see. Not knowing what might be happening, or whom he could ask, he followed Jasper at a distance.

At the river's edge, Jasper took the rope about the animal's neck and led it into the water so that its forelegs were almost covered. The ox lowed once again and touched its nose to the surface but, strangely, did not drink.

Suddenly the ax swung. There was a flash of metal, the thud of a blow, and then, as Dan strained to see, the ox slowly slid into the water, the front legs going down first, its low moan cut off by the current, and a dark puddle of red spread slowly out over the water.

"The devil in you!" Jasper cried out, then turned and wiped the ax on the grass.

SHAKING, DAN WAITED until there were sounds outside the cottage and people were about before he returned. He dared not stay another night, he knew. Something had occurred that he did not understand, some ritualistic slaughter, and he felt in his bones that

113

had he been found asleep in the barn, it would have been he who now floated down the Ouse. Somehow he must get Orlenda off to herself and persuade her to leave York with him immediately.

As it turned out, however, there was no secret made of the slaughter.

"The ox was killed this morning," Ambrose told him as he came hesitantly into the clearing where the family drank their morning brew. "The pestilence had got it, and we feared for the sheep and the pigs."

It was an explanation Dan had not considered, and he felt somewhat reassured. But there was an unnaturalness in the air that bothered him, and even Rachel, sitting across the fire with Orlenda, gave him no smile. He looked into Orlenda's face, trying to read her eyes, but all he saw was worry. And when she saw him looking at her, she dropped her eyes. Nor was he able to get a clue from Nat, for he had turned himself sideways and sat looking off toward the river.

Panic raced through him again, and he stood staring at the group. Rose mechanically stirred the breakfast gruel, saying nothing. Only Jasper's eyes met his, and they were so dark, so hostile, that only fear held Dan to his spot, fear that if he ran, he would hear the whir of an ax behind him and feel it cleave his back.

"Perhaps it is time, as you said, to leave here," Ambrose told him. "Old William is dead this morning, his body up there on the road. There is death all about us now."

Dan was stunned with the news, both their willingness to leave and the death of their neighbor. His pulse leaped with the thought that perhaps Ambrose had mellowed in his opinion of him, but his heart advised caution. There were Jasper's eyes to contend with. It was all too easy, somehow.

He looked again at Orlenda, then Nat, and his uneasiness grew. What had they all talked about in his absence? Or was it just as Ambrose had said—the death of the ox and Old William that had changed their minds?

"I have decided to send my daughters to the country," Ambrose went on. "With Old William gone, his sheep will wander about unfed, his pigs will root in the garden. The rest of us will stay to look after the place. This is our home, our fields, and only God knows which of us will live to see tomorrow. There is a chance to take on leaving and a chance to take if we stay. If we divide up the family, perhaps there will be someone left to remember. . . ."

Dan listened without answering, afraid that his voice would reveal his misgivings.

"If it suits you," Ambrose went on, "you may go with them, and I will entrust them to your care. Perhaps in a few weeks, when the planting is over, I will send one of my sons to join you."

It was all that Dan had hoped, and yet there was a sadness about Orlenda's face he could not understand. Perhaps only grief at leaving her parents, he told himself. How could he expect her to feel otherwise?

"Are you hungry?" Ambrose asked him. "Would you have gruel?"

Dan shook his head, not trusting his lips to move.

"Then I've a request to make of you, Daniel. Go into town and ask for the gray sentry who guards Monk Bar. When you find him, tell him that Ambrose Faw, his old friend, requests the use of two horses, that he would send his daughters away where they might be safe."

Dan tried to understand the request, tried to connect it to the expressions on the faces around him, tried to read its meaning in Orlenda's eyes, but she would not look at him directly. Why did Ambrose not ask for the horses himself? Was it wise to send a stranger? What if the sentry said no?

"Perhaps he will have need of his horses," Dan said finally.

"He is a sentry," Ambrose replied. "He would never leave his post."

Still Dan hesitated. "How will he know I come from you? Why would he trust his horses to a stranger?"

Ambrose reached under the belt of his tunic and took out a small purse. From the purse he took a coin. "Give him this coin, and he will know you come from me."

There, in his hand, lay the Roman denarius.

THE ICY CHILL that had bored through Dan's hand when he took the coin had now enveloped his heart.

He had tied the denarius up in the hem of his tunic, but it seemed to weigh on his soul.

He could hardly refuse to go. One of the horses would be used by him, and it was only right that he go to fetch them. Why, then, was he so hesitant? Why did he feel it to be a trap? What was the meaning of the look in Orlenda's eyes back there by the cottage, and Nat's face, turned away?

He reached the road above the path and turned toward the walls of the city. He had not gone fifty yards when he saw the body of the neighbor, sprawled in the dirt as Ambrose had said. Dan gasped and drew back, as though the stench were a tangible thing, grasping at him, choking him, squeezing the last wisp of air from his lungs.

Old William's body was bloated, the stomach distended, the wrists and ankles swollen. His tunic had been half torn off by dogs who, sensing the unnaturalness of the death, had since run off. Huge dark splotches covered the skin, making one entire leg seem black, and under one arm, which had been thrown over his head, was a lump as large as an apple. There were others on his neck and on his groin, and some had burst, issuing a dark substance that had trickled on down his body and left small pools of dried black in the dirt. Only two days before Dan had sat beside this man, and though Old William may have had some symptoms even then, he had not looked unwell.

Now Dan could indeed believe the reports that

people who had seemingly been in the best of health in the morning had been found dead by evening. Covering his mouth, he hurried around the corpse and began to run. His feet felt numb as they hit the pebbles, as though there were no sensation, as though his ankles ended in nothingness. Spasms of panic seemed to grip him at the back of his neck. Behind him the Faws waited, before him the walls of York; on one side of him the River, and on the other— death: a body here, a dog there, a horse on the ground, its sides heaving. Up on the hills lay the corpses of sheep and not even the birds would go near them.

He thought for a moment of bolting—of going in one gate of the city and out the other. He thought of climbing down the bank to the Ouse and waiting for a boat to come along, begging to be taken aboard. Then he thought of Orlenda again, and his head ached with confusion. He longed to see her free of this place, longed to take her away, but the look in her eyes had dismayed him. If this was a trap, she had let him go. Was it better to risk it, with the possibility that he might yet save her, or should he trust the rising terror in his chest and leave now, alone, while he could? Hadn't Nat himself once urged him to leave? As a friend, he had said, he was telling Dan he should go.

And yet, the thought of the girl. . . . Would she have nursed him so long if she did not care for him? Did she deserve no trust? His feet went on, powered not by resolve but by ambivalence. Unable to decide, he went ahead, and a few minutes later passed under the portcullis at Bootham Bar.

It was a different York this time than it had been only two days before. In those two days, May had turned to June, and at every turn in the streets, at every other window, it seemed, was the stink of death. Here and there a body had been placed on a doorstep, some wrapped in burial cloths, others half-dressed with flies swarming about their erupted boils. There were no hawkers this day, no sellers of strawberries. The silence was broken only by the howl of dogs, running unattended in packs, and the squeaky cart of the gravediggers as they went on their gruesome rounds, picking up the dead and throwing the corpses on the growing heap.

Shutters and doors were closed tightly, as if to keep out the sights and smells. No children played in the doorways, no mothers lounged on the steps, and when an occasional tradesman hurried by, he invariably crossed to the other side to avoid whatever contagion there might be.

The gray sentry, Ambrose had told him, could be found in a guardhouse beside Monk Bar. If not there, then on duty on the wall itself.

Dan paused on Goodramgate, across the street from the doctor's house. It occurred to him that he knew only one other person in York beside the Faws, and that was the physician's wife. Perhaps she would know the gray sentry and whether or not he was a man to be trusted. Perhaps Dan could simply tell her all that had happened and hope that—as the wife of an educated man—she would understand his predicament and counsel him.

As he stared over at the house, deciding what to do, a second gravedigger appeared from around the corner, pushing his cart. He wheeled it up to the door of the physician's house and stopped. There were no dead on this cart, only an old man, lying on his side, moaning piteously, the telltale marks of the pestilence on his skin. Leaving the man unattended, the gravedigger went up to the door of the house and banged loudly, an official-looking paper in his hand. When a minute or two had gone by, he shouted an order that he must be admitted at once, and banged again.

This time the door opened, revealing a figure draped in a shawl, hiding the face. Dan could not see who it was—a servant, perhaps? The person was holding something—a glass box, it appeared to be— and was showing the gravedigger its contents, thrusting it toward him and drawing back, attempting to close the door again. But the gravedigger reached out and grasped the arm of the hooded woman, and when at last she was seated beside the moaning man, the cart went on. As it rounded the corner, however, the figure swayed, and Dan caught a glimpse of red hair beneath the shawl. He sprang forward, then stopped, realizing there was nothing he could do. The gravedigger had his orders.

He leaned against a doorway as the cart disappeared, his terror accompanied by nausea. The doctor's wife—she too had been taken and was on her way to a plague-house. The gravedigger would be back before nightfall, Dan felt sure, to plunder the house while it was empty. Where was the doctor? Where was the town crier, or the village watch? Everywhere the streets seemed to have been taken over by dogs.

A woman leaned out a window above and shouted for Dan to move on—that two men dying on her doorstep were enough and she'd not have a third.

Dan stumbled out to the street again where Monk Bar rose up before him, its high walls towering above its arch, the cruciform slits on either side like narrow eyes, watching.

The dread gripped him. It pressed against his chest, chilled his hands, and made his back clammy with perspiration. He felt sure that he was walking to his own death and that the denarius, when he presented it, would seal his fate. Yet still he went on, and Monk Bar loomed larger and larger, its archway a gaping mouth to swallow him up. Terrified now that his resolve would give way or that his knees would buckle, he suddenly lunged forward, rushed up to the door of the guardhouse along the wall, and banged on it with both fists. Then he reached down and untied the denarius from the hem of his tunic and waited.

He was conscious, as he did so, how motley and

unkempt he looked. There was straw on his clothes and in his hair. His tunic was filthy, and there was mud from the riverbank on his feet. A fine impression he would make on the sentry.

But there was no sound from inside. Nothing. He remembered Ambrose's instructions and turned toward the gate itself.

There were stairs in the thick stone wall leading to the story above, and Dan entered the dank, dark passageway and began his slow ascent, his teeth chattering as though with a chill, the denarius like ice in the palm of his hand.

There was no sound in the tower but the wind. He had not noticed it below on the street, but here in the imposing stone gateway, what breeze there was was channeled and compressed through the narrow passages until it seemed to whistle past his ears and whip the tunic about his legs.

His footsteps echoed on the stone steps beneath him, and their very sound made him realize how alone he was here, how hidden from view. Sweat poured off his forehead. Perhaps there was no gray sentry. Perhaps no one at all. Perhaps he had been followed by Jasper or Ambrose himself, and once he reached the inner parts of the bar, where his screams would be muffled, they would rush him from behind.

He came to the room on the second story and found it empty. The huge windlass with iron ratchet and pawl, which raised and lowered the spiked portcullis, stood against one wall. On the other side of the room was a narrow stone archway with a curved staircase leading to the story above.

Dan stood still, listening, his ears straining for the slightest noise. Then he called out, "I've come to see the gray sentry."

His words ricocheted against the sweeping arch of the ceiling to smack against the cold stone of the opposite wall and rebound, shattering the stillness. He waited, holding his breath, then crossed the floor and began to climb up to the floor above.

There was a noise behind him, like a door opening, a quick thud of feet, and then, as he turned, he saw a figure lunge into the archway below. A hand encircled his ankle. A moment later he was pinned against the stone wall of the staircase, then pressed down upon the steps, and he felt the cold of a knife blade at his throat. The assailant rose up before him, and he found himself staring into the face of Joe Stanton.

7

WHAT ARE YOU doing here? Who sent you?"
The blade pressed harder against his
neck. Dan felt the perspiration trickling
down his back, yet his body trembled.

"I'm looking for the gray sentry," he said. His
lips were so dry that they stuck together.

"Speak up!" the man said, clutching Dan more
tightly.

"The gray sentry," Dan said, as the edge of a
stone step cut into his back. He recognized the gray
hair, the gray face. . . . Except for the steel blue eyes,
Joe Stanton always had a gray look about him, like a
man made of fog.

"And now that you've found him, what then?"
the sentry said, and Dan stared. "You are a scum of
the swamps. You live off the dying—once when you
cart them away and again when you put them under.
The taste of carrion is there on your lips. I can smell
it on your breath."

Dan started to protest, but the sentry knocked his head against the wall to silence him.

"I have raised this nephew as my own," he breathed through clenched teeth. "I taught him to shoot an arrow, to train a falcon, to fish the pond and the river. Now you would take him from me, sick as he is, and carry him off to a plague-house."

"I only—"

"You would only ask payment to let him stay here with me, I know. And then, after pocketing your bribe, you would send another digger around to carry the boy away. You are the dregs in a cup, the foot of a swine, the pus of a boil."

"I'm Daniel the Scribe," Dan managed to gulp finally, "sent by Ambrose Faw."

The steel blue eyes seemed to grow darker moment by moment. The face froze, as though the expression had been sculpted upon it. Then slowly the sentry relaxed his grip. Pulling Dan back down the stairs and into the light of the gatehouse room, he stood him in the center of the floor and looked him over.

"How am I to believe this? What do you give me for proof?"

Dan held out the Roman denarius and Joe took it, then let go of Dan's tunic. For a long time he looked at the coin, then at Dan, and finally said,

"I am Joseph, the gray sentry." He made no apology for his error, gave no explanation. Nor did his eyes soften. But he put his knife back in the sheath at his side and motioned Dan over to a bench along one wall.

Still short of breath, his heart pounding fiercely, Dan sat down, rubbing his neck where the strong hand had grasped it. Across the room on either side of the windlass were two small doors he had over-looked before. One, from which the man had come, was slightly ajar. He looked into Joe Stanton's eyes and wondered how it could be that he recognized his old friend, yet Joe did not seem to know him at all.

"I gave you no reason to suspect me," Dan said, and anger seeped out along with his words. He was too exhausted to be frightened any longer. He did not know if he merely imagined it or whether a faint smile played about the lips of the sentry.

"You gave me every reason," Joseph said. "You stood pounding below on the door of the guard-house. You came walking unbidden up the stairs to Monk Bar. You bellowed out my name for all to hear, and you look as though you spent the night in a barn."

"I did," Dan said simply. "I've neither eaten nor bathed, but I had no intention of doing you harm. I came with a request from Ambrose."

"What does he ask of me?"

"He would like to send his daughters away from York, today if possible. The grandmother died, then the ox, then a neighbor. Ambrose asks, as a friend, for the use of two horses."

The sentry studied him carefully, his eyes riveted to Dan's face. For a full minute they watched each other, waiting. Finally Joseph said, "Why did you bother to bring the denarius to me? You could have traded it for shillings in the shops. Are you so fond of Ambrose?"

"I'm fond of his daughter."

"Ahhhh."

"I'd like to see her go where there has been no disease, where she might have a chance. I've only recently recovered from the pestilence myself."

"So you are Daniel the Scribe—the recovered?"

"Yes."

"Ah. A miracle was worked on you then. But you ask a miracle of me. I have already loaned out one of my horses and there is only the other one left, a young horse, not nearly as strong as the first."

"You won't need it yourself?"

"I have a job to do here."

Dan watched him, his heart pounding. "Would you allow Ambrose this favor, then?"

Again the gray sentry's eyes seemed to be boring through Dan's forehead into his brain.

"The horse rides only two. How would you decide who is to go and who to stay?"

Dan was not sure. The girls could ride and he could walk, but then their journey would be considerably slower. They needed to get as far away as possible, as fast as they could. Ambrose would not send his daughters off to the country alone, he was sure of it. Nor could Dan bear the thought of Orlenda going without him.

"The daughters would be given the horse," Dan told him at last, "But it wouldn't be wise to send them out in the countryside alone."

"You are right, of course. There are robbers at every turn."

"Isn't it possible for this horse to ride three?" Dan pleaded. "One of the daughters is small and light —a child of seven."

"You ask for my horse, and as if that were not enough, you would burden it down."

"No, I promise you. We would take only what needed to go."

"You would add four and then five, and the horse would die along the road."

"I give you my word there will be only three."

"I give you my horse and you give me your word. Have you nothing better than that?"

"We have given you the Roman denarius."

The sentry's eyes blazed. "Do you think a horse is worth nothing more than a denarius? Is the use of my horse not worth infinitely more than a coin?"

"I had thought you were doing it for Ambrose, for friendship's sake."

"But it is not Ambrose, strangely, who does the pleading, it is you. What have you to give me, of yourself, if I am to save this girl you love?"

It was as though all his life had come together at this moment. As though every minute Dan had lived,

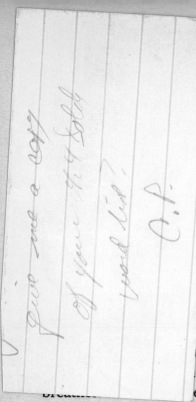

Give me a copy of your title / word list? O.P.

d loved, existed for this dot
ne life of the universe. As
for this, would die for this,
helped Orlenda to live, he
uccessfully.

the sentry that was unique?
hat he alone could do? He
protested. To have come all
d what he did, to have seen
. . .

have a nephew sick with the
ly. "And you know it's forbid-
, that you should keep him
spread to you."

," the sentry said coldly.

the disease and recovered, let
d to him for as long as he
e go, and I'll be back before
evening. That I can promise you."

For a long time the sentry did not answer. As he
looked into the man's face, it seemed to Dan that the
steel blue eyes turned gray, then black, as though
pools of consciousness and unconsciousness were
crashing together, as though history were playing out
scenes before him—scenes that had been and those
that were yet to be. Was it possible that finally, in this
moment, the sentry had some dim recollection that
he had met this scribe before—that they would, in
some distant time, be friends?

Joseph stood up abruptly. "Take the horse," he

said, "and I will see you here again before dusk. Tell Ambrose that my horse is his for as long as he has need of it." He bent down and slipped the Roman denarius into his shoe.

"Should I stop in at the doctor's," Dan suggested, "for a preventive draught for you?"

"The doctor himself is dead," the sentry replied. "There is none to tend us now but ourselves."

HE RODE ALONG PETERGATE, out Bootham Bar and back down the road. He could not describe his emotions, could not seem to gauge how he felt. He had been sent for two horses and was returning with only one—a young one at that. Nat would go with Orlenda and Rachel, he felt sure. That was the way it should be. He himself would remain behind. He knew that his life was in danger in York, that there were many, like Jasper, who resented his recovery, and yet . . . and yet . . . he would stay.

Dan wanted to get hold of the sadness he knew was there—wanted to grip it, feel it, taste it fully, and have done with it before it overtook him later. But he could not sort it out. It was mixed inexplicably with a strange feeling of exhilaration.

"I may never see her again," he said aloud, hoping to bring his emotions into focus.

The pain deepened and the sadness was sharpened, but there was something more he could not understand. As nearly as he could describe it, as irrational as it seemed, the feeling was joy.

How can this be? he asked himself. How had he achieved it? By what trick, what illusion, could he possibly think of himself as happy? How could he even persuade himself that he had saved Orlenda's life, when she could fall ill tomorrow or the day after that and die without his ever knowing? What had he to look forward to now but nursing duty in the gatehouse, attending a sick child in a room of stench and black-tainted vomit? At any moment he might be attacked by a mob intent upon finding the cause of their own misfortune. He could be butchered before he even got back.

He examined his joy. He spread it out before him in his mind, turned it, shook it, wrestled with it, but it would not go away. Like a lungful of fresh air, it seemed to make him lighter, to lift him slightly off the horse, to make his heart beat faster with an aliveness he had not felt for a long time.

He was living under a risk, but this itself made his life more precious, his accomplishments more meaningful, even if no one else knew it but he. It was indeed possible, he decided, for a person living under such odds, such uncertainties, to live his life well, regardless of how much time he was given.

What a miracle it was that he—or anyone else—had been born at all, he mused; he had been only one of four hundred million spermatozoa, all racing for the ovum, but he was the one who had made it. He lived. Even if he accomplished nothing, his life was a miracle. All life was a miracle, and those who spent their years never knowing that were the ones who missed out. Anything at all that he accomplished beyond breathing, therefore, was a cause for wonder. Why had he never realized this before? Why did he feel so elated now, so complete?

He was doing what he had come to do, he was giving Orlenda a chance. He could not give her a guarantee, but for the first time she would be free to go where she pleased, stopped by no soldiers, detained in no city, a daughter of the countryside. Her chance might last only a few days or months or years, but it was he who had bargained for it, sacrificed for it, and in doing so had given his own life purpose. He did not understand how it was so, but the joy was there.

Old William's body had been taken by the time he reached the path, and as he started down the slope toward the cottage, the joy was clouded over by his obligation to the Faws. What would they say when they saw that he had succeeded in only half of his mission? What if Nat did not want to leave now, or Ambrose would not let him go? It was Dan who was supposed to take the girls so that their brothers could plant the fields.

He rode slowly into the clearing, and a cold finger of panic raced through him, sliding down his throat and settling in his lungs. They were sitting about as he had left them, their faces expectant, waiting.

Ambrose got up and came out to meet him.

There was something in his expression that Dan had never seen before, something in his eyes that made Dan pause, something in the clasp of his large hand over Dan's there on the reins that made him look about wonderingly. It was as though he had been on a long journey, and they were welcoming him home.

Rose came over with a bowl of leek soup.

"Come now and eat," she said. "You've had nothing in your stomach, and your head will suffer for it. Here. Jasper will tend to the horse."

"I couldn't get the second one," Dan said quickly, climbing down, afraid they had misunderstood. "Joseph had loaned it out already. But he has given permission for this horse to ride three, since Rachel is light."

"You have done well to bring us one," Ambrose said, and motioned to the food. "Eat! Eat! The day is early, and you have a long journey ahead of you."

Orlenda smiled at him from across the yard, and he saw that she had put her belongings in a cloth bag, ready to go. How could he tell her that he was not going with her? He tried to eat, but his appetite failed him. Jasper was grooming the horse, patting its side and rubbing it down, and Nat was fastening Orlenda's bag to its back.

At last Dan said, "I made an agreement in order to get the horse; the gray sentry's nephew has been taken ill, and the sentry would keep him out of a plague-house. I've promised to stay and tend him as long as he is alive."

Orlenda turned slowly and looked at him.

"Ah," said Ambrose. "So that's it."

"I wanted to go with Orlenda," Dan said earnestly. "With all my heart, I'd hoped to go with the girls and watch over them on the road. But the pestilence, it seems, will not touch me again, and someone else should have my chance. Perhaps Nat. . . ."

"I'll go, then," Nat said. "They can't be out on the road alone. We'll go as far as the town of Ripon, Daniel, and perhaps you'll find us later. It's been said that the Archbishop himself spends the summer there. We've been given the name of Boswell, a herdsman, who will take us in. If the sickness comes, we'll push on to Scotland. Or perhaps, if the danger passes, we'll return here."

He walked over and embraced Dan. "You have proven yourself a friend, Daniel. Surely your coming was a good thing."

RACHEL WAS SKIPPING in and out of the house, placing a few possessions on the ground, deciding what would go and what would stay, seemingly oblivious of what the separation might mean.

"Will you walk to the river with me once more while the horse is fed?" Orlenda said to Dan, and Ambrose, sitting on the step, watched them go. Down the path, Dan put one arm about her, and she laid her head on his shoulder.

"I'll miss you, Orlenda," he told her.

"And I you, Daniel." She slipped her arm around

his waist, and then suddenly her face was against his chest and she was sobbing violently, clutching his tunic. He let her cry, his face against her hair, stroking her gently.

At last she straightened up, wiping her eyes, and tried to smile. "I should be happy you are alive. When you left this morning, I wondered if I would ever see you again—whether the gray sentry would send you back to us at all."

"What do you mean?"

"When my father gave you the coin, I knew it was to be your test. I hoped that you would pass it, prayed for you, believed that you would, but still I wondered: what if the sentry misjudged you? What then?"

"I don't understand. What are you talking about?"

"Nat told you once about my father and his fortune—about the old priestess, descended from Druids, who predicted that one day there would come into his life a young buck, who would change it for either ill or good. . . ."

"Yes, I remember. And he thought perhaps I was the one. . . ."

"But there's more. My father and Joseph have been friends since they were children. Well, friends and yet not friends. My father is a freeman. He belongs to no lord, gives allegiance to no master, and has long resisted our wars against the Scots, his own people. He was against the Battle of Crécy as well, for the French have sided with the Scots against the British. So he has no particular love for York. It is the land itself he loves, the rivers, the sky, the air . . . and he doesn't feel that any king or country has the right to lay claim to them, that they belong to all people. It would be against all that he ever lived and breathed to take a man's life at the command of a king. Joseph, though, is bound by duty, and he would defend his king to the death, even against his own conscience. To him, duty is the noblest virtue. But as I said, they have been friends of a sort since childhood, and Joseph's fortune, it turns out, was the same as my father's. Moreover, the priestess predicted that whatever happened to one of them would happen to the other as well. When they found they had a common destiny, they put aside their differences. The misfortune or the destruction of one, they knew, meant the destruction of both. And so they made an oath."

They had reached the bank of the river, and sat down together, Dan intent on her story.

"There is a Roman denarius that passes between them. Whenever one feels that perhaps the young buck of which the fortune spoke has come, he sends him to the other for his decision, whether the young man has come for ill or for good. The denarius is their sign. This young man is sent to the other, either carrying the coin and asking a favor, or asking for the denarius itself. If it is decided by the other that the young man bodes good, the favor is granted or the denarius given to him to carry back to the other. If it appears that he is not the young buck at all, the favor is denied."

"And if it is decided that he is the young buck who will change their lives for ill?"

She did not answer for a moment. "I don't know. It has never happened yet, and I would hate to think what my father might do. So far, the few that have come along have been common. But you . . . I have always known, since first I saw you, that you were special—that you had come to us for a reason, and I prayed that it would be for good."

"And so I have passed the test?"

"Joseph would not have sent you with the horse if you hadn't. I don't know what passed between you and the gray sentry, but I know that whatever it was you spoke, you spoke it well. I only wish you were coming, too. You have given us hope, Daniel. It was you who sat by Granny at the last when none of us could tend her. Against my father's suspicions and Jasper's ill-temper, you've stayed and proven yourself a friend. Oh, Daniel, I wish you were going with us. Is it wrong of me, do you think, to wish so to live, to want to see my sister grow up into a healthy young woman?"

Dan held her to him. "No, Orlenda. All of us feel the same. Everyone wishes to live. Why should you not say it?"

"If there were something I could do here if my parents or brothers were to fall ill, I would stay.

There would be no question. Even at the risk of my own life, I would stay and do what I could. But when those who are well can do nothing to help the sick—when we are told to keep away from them, even—it would be more than I could ever bear. I wish, sometimes, that the old Druid priestess had told my fortune—mine and Rachel's. I wish I knew how it will end."

They were quiet for a while, and then Orlenda said, "He has a gift, this Joseph. He sees things we do not see, hears things we do not hear, and knows of things that happened a long time ago, as though he had once lived in another time."

Did it all come together, then? Was there a reason why Joe Stanton returned again and again to a life he might have lived once before? Was he sent as a guide, perhaps, through the perils of times past, so that Dan could more courageously accept the uncertainty of his own future?

Orlenda went on. "I asked him once how he could stand to spend his life on a wall, always watching for the worst—the vandal hordes, the armies, the fires, the floods. But he said that he watches for good as well—for kings riding up from London, the Archbishop coming down from the north, the messengers galloping through the gates, or merchant ships coming up the Ouse from the sea." She turned to him suddenly and said, "It was I who brought the pestilence, you know."

"*You*, Orlenda?"

"Yes, I'm sure of it. When Nat went off to war, I thought to myself that nothing could be as terrible as men fighting each other—men who had never met, who were sent at the command of kings when perhaps they would rather be at home plowing their fields. I heard of the horrible new weapon, the English longbow, and something else called gunpowder, which could shoot out explosions. Mother had a vision. She said the war would last a hundred years, and I could not bear the thought of it. My children and their children and all the children yet to come, fighting and dying. And so I prayed for a huge calamity that would strike all countries alike—that would threaten all men everywhere, whether kings or commoners—a calamity so great that people would forget about war and killing and would all join together."

She put her face down in her skirt and shook her head. "It didn't happen that way at all, God forgive me. Cities closed their gates against strangers, seaports turned away foreign ships, mothers abandoned their children, and husbands left their wives. I have heard all the stories. It was a dreadful thing that I wished for, and I wish now that Christ had never heard me at all."

"It was not pain you really wished for, Orlenda, it was peace," Dan said gently, "and that's a noble wish. You had nothing more to do with the pestilence than the planets or seas or tides."

She gently stroked his hand. "You comfort me,

Daniel. You're like Joseph sometimes—a sentry for hope. I'll try to remember that when things around us are awful. I'll think of the gray sentry there on the wall and realize that perhaps even then, he sees something coming that will change everything."

"What we need," Dan mused aloud, "is a new Columbus."

She looked at him strangely. "What is that, Daniel? A columbus?"

He smiled. "Something that is yet to be."

"You talk so strangely, Daniel. You know many things, have been many places. I have been nowhere. . . ."

"That makes no difference."

"I'm speaking truly. Our lives have been very different. But you have changed mine, and no matter where I go—Scotland, even—I'll think of you and love you. . . ."

"Orlenda. . . ."

She placed one finger on his lips. "I feel like a bird that once had a broken wing. You have healed me and now I can fly. Some day, perhaps, I will come to you in disguise." She laughed delightedly with the thought of it. "Some day I may come to you as a bird with a broken wing, and when I do, be good to me."

They walked back to the clearing together. The horse stood waiting.

Nat bid his parents goodbye and clutched his brother's hand. "Are you sure you would not go in my place?"

Jasper shook his head and helped him mount. "You've been through too much already, Nat. War has robbed you of a good leg, and you shouldn't gamble your life as well. I'll come to Ripon later, perhaps, for the horse, and ask at Boswell's for you. Perhaps, in a few months' time, a year, even, we will all be together again. Godspeed."

He lifted Orlenda and then Rachel onto the horse in front of Nat. Sensing the separation at last. Rachel bent down and kissed her mother, then the horse turned and started slowly up toward the road.

Ambrose did not watch the leave-taking. It was bad luck, he said, to say goodbye. Bowing his head, the gray-black beard flowing down onto his chest, he turned toward the house and stood leaning against the doorframe with one large hand until the sound of hooves had faded away. As Dan watched them go, only Nat's back was visible from behind and, fluttering out from one side, the fragile edge of Orlenda's shawl.

THE SMALL ROOM in the turret was stuffy and hot in the days that followed. The sentry's young nephew lay listlessly on a pallet on the stone floor as Dan came and went, bringing cold cloths to place on his forehead, to wipe up the vomit, or to catch the foul black spittle that issued from his lips.

Each day Dan changed the straw upon which the youth lay, and each day the boy grew weaker still. Dan cooked a gruel on a brick stove in the guardhouse and carried it up the stairs to the turret, but each day the boy drank less and less. And all the while Joseph, the sentry, paced back and forth on the wall in a rigid exercise of grief.

Birds came and sang at the cruciform window. Carts rumbled through the arch underneath. Bells, which were no longer allowed to toll each death for fear of depressing the survivors, rang out whenever there was the slightest cause for celebration. But the young boy on the straw seemed to hear nothing, see nothing, feel nothing. And finally, one evening, he died.

Dan washed the body with clean water and rolled it up in a shroud. All night he sat with the boy while the gray sentry walked the wall, and it seemed that in those footsteps Dan could hear the beat of a heart, the tick of a clock, the passing of minutes and hours.

In the morning, before the dark had lifted, when mists were rising from the countryside, forming a wall beyond the wall of York, Dan and Joseph carried the frail body down the winding stairs, through the heart of the city, and down the bank to the river.

Gently, gently, they waded out together, and when they were standing in water up to their thighs, they released their hold on the boy. The current picked him up and bore him slowly toward the east, where, leaving the city behind, he would continue his journey on to the River Humber and then on out to the sea.

They were facing each other there in the water,

Dan and Joseph, veiled in the fog that rose up around them.

"I'm glad that you came," Joseph told him. "All who live in these times are special to each other. We are a different breed, a different sort, to carry on as we have done with death all about us. Write down what you have seen and heard, so that others may know what it is to live with fear. Write so that those who come after, if there are any left, will know what it was like to be in York at this time—when the seas rose up and the stars crossed and the planets conspired against us."

Yes, he would do that, Dan decided. He would write that men had looked to the sky for the cause of their misfortune. They had blamed the air and the stars and the sun. And all the while, it was the lowly rat.

He started suddenly, remembering something else—something he had studied in school. No, it was not the rat at all, but the fleas upon the rat. Because of a certain flea, armies had crumbled, cities had been deserted, and brave men had fled in panic. People had looked outward for the root of their misery, to the heavens and beyond, and all the time it was there in their houses, in their beds, upon their bodies. They had carried it, unknowingly, next to their hearts.

"It's the flea, Joseph!" Dan said to the man before him.

Yet his voice made no sound. His lips moved, but he did not speak. He reached out his hand but found himself drifting away, being separated from his friend by the rising current. Desperately he stretched out his arm, and Joseph in turn stretched his, but their fingers did not touch. Wider and wider grew the space between them, thicker and thicker the mist, until finally the gray sentry was but a blur on the surface of the water and there was a whole river between them.

8

DARKNESS AND DAMP and the icy shroud of swirling water. Flashes of light, of heat, mingled with mists and vapors. Swell of the river, swell of time, currents connecting, blending, severing, until he was tossed at last on the bank.

He lay there unhurt, strangely refreshed, looking about for Joseph—wanting to say something more about his nephew. He wanted to say that friendship is never wasted, even when it is cut short—that in the brief span of time in which the sentry had raised his nephew, Joseph had enriched both their lives.

But Joseph was not there. He had disappeared as surely as the walls of York and the river itself. Instead, Dan found himself lying beside a stream, and the morning sun was just beginning to sift through the branches above, spotting his face with warmth.

He sat up on one elbow and stared at his clothes.

Gone were the slippers and tunic that Orlenda had given him. In their place he wore his old pair of jeans with the frayed pocket, the faded shirt, the boots, and there—around his waist—the belt with the eagle buckle. He scrambled to his feet, his mouth open, touching the buckle, examining it; then wheeled around, looking for Oriole. How could this be? He had made no trade that he could remember.

They had been at this spot, and it was here that the coin had fallen into the water. But the bank was deserted.

He had not slept. He knew that as surely as he knew his own skin. What had happened had not been the wild imaginings of a restless dream. He walked along the bank, searching for the path leading to the clearing above. It was then that he heard his name:

"Dan!"

It was a familiar voice, but not Oriole's.

"Dan."

The sound of it trailed off, as though the caller's head had turned. Then suddenly,

"Dan, it's you!"

He wheeled about. There, making her way along the bank of the stream, was Blossom, her heavy ankles thrust in a pair of black overshoes, her apron hiked up about her waist so as not to catch on the bushes. Her face dissolved in relief.

"Dan, *lad!*" she sputtered, half-scolding. "You scared the very life out of me!"

He went toward her hesitatingly, not knowing what to say, unsure of how long he had been gone or what had happened in his absence. He remembered the time in the cellar when Blossom had found him lying by the spring and all the questions it had produced. He could not risk upsetting her so again.

"I didn't think you'd worry, Bee," he said. "I thought you'd figure I was camping out."

She looked at him incredulously. "Camping out?" She wheeled around, staring at the bank. "Just camping out in your clothes, Dan?"

He shrugged, still groping with the effort of adjusting to this time, this place.

The incredulity on her face gave way to exasperation. "Dan Roberts!" The words came tumbling out as though she could scarcely control herself. "I went to bed last night thinking you'd be back any minute, and when I discovered you were still gone this morning, I was so worried I called your father. I didn't know what else to do. He's on his way down from Harrisburg this very minute."

All that had happened, then, had occurred in the space of a single night?

"You shouldn't have worried, Bee." He looked about in confusion. "But where are they? Where did they go?"

"Who, lad?"

"The gypsies. I told you I was going out to find them."

"That was my own foolishness, Dan. Old Mr. Gallagher dropped by for a few minutes last night after you left. He's been burning brush over beyond the woods there, and it was his smoke we saw above the trees. All my talk of gypsies was just this old heart longing for their return, I guess. I sent you on a wild goose chase, that's what I did."

"They were here, Bee!"

"Now, Dan, don't you tell me what I know with my own head. Mr. Gallagher told me himself—no one's set foot in these woods but a tramp or two for the past ten, fifteen years. That's likely what you saw."

He stared at her. "But the old gypsy—the one you told me about—who came to the house asking for coins."

"You know what I think? I think he was just passing through with a carnival or something. That's what Mr. Gallagher says."

Dan knew better than to argue with her. He would go back to the house, reassure his father, and then—when the uproar died down—come back and look for Oriole.

They walked single file, Dan behind his grandmother, putting out one hand occasionally to steady her where the ground was rocky, listening to the familiar grunting and puffing.

"Lord, Dan, what am I going to say to your father now when he shows up? A mercy your mother wasn't home, for no telling how she'd take it. She's got final exams all this week, Brian said. They don't need any more worries, that's certain."

"I'm really sorry, Bee. I figured you'd know I'd be okay."

"Like as not you would, but what if you slipped and hit your head on a rock or something? What if you fell face down in the stream? You going to camp out, you *tell* me next time, you hear? What am I supposed to think, waking up this morning and finding you gone? My old heart won't take all this mucking about. I've not even had my tea yet, and Lord, there's the cow to be milked and—"

He gave her a swat on the backside. "Hush, Bee, I said I'm sorry, didn't I? I'll milk the cow, apologize to Dad, fix your tea, and never go out at night again if you'll just quit yammering at me."

It was not that he was feeling so playful. But he wanted quiet about him now. He wanted to let his mind explore what had happened, to drink in the sensations of being back, to wonder at the ways he had changed, yet not changed at all.

"Well, all right, but you're old enough, Dan, not to worry me like that," Blossom said, and then she kept still.

He half expected to see the thatch-roofed cottage when he reached the south pasture. He almost expected to see Orlenda walking about the yard, scattering bread crumbs for the geese, to see Ambrose leading the ox into the barn, or Jasper sitting there on the stump.

But it was Blossom's house, surely—the barn and the shed—and there, in the driveway behind Blossom's old Ford, his father's Plymouth.

HE WAS STANDING in the kitchen when they walked in, hands thrust in his pockets, shoulders hunched, face turned toward the front door, waiting. He wheeled around when he heard the back screen open, and then he was coming toward them, arms outstretched. He hugged Blossom, then Dan.

"Now what's this all about?" Mr. Roberts said. "A wonder I didn't get a ticket the way I raced down here!" He held Dan out away from him and looked him over. "A little thin around the face, but otherwise you *look* okay. What happened?"

Blossom grunted. "You'll not hear it from me. *Yammering* at him, he says!"

She glared at Dan crossly, then her old face began to fold itself into a smile. "Oh, sit down, you two, while I make us a proper breakfast. Brian, it's *good* to have you here at the table again."

Dan sat opposite his father, and they studied each other. He was aware once again of how much alike they were—same long fingers, same oval face, same hairline, lips. . . . Mr. Roberts looked healthy enough. His hands rested lightly on top of the table and did not appear to shake. He was waiting, Dan knew, for an explanation.

"I should have told Bee I might sleep out," Dan began. "I was preoccupied. Wanted to sort things through. I just didn't think."

"Didn't take a sleeping bag with you?"

"No, I just stretched out on the grass. It was a good night. I'm okay."

Mr. Roberts didn't say anything for a while—just sat there watching him, while Blossom bustled about the stove.

"How do you feel now?" he asked finally.

"It's strange," Dan said, letting a little of it spill out, "but it's as though I've been away for a long, long time." He sat watching his glass fill with milk as Blossom poured from the pitcher. "I just had to get my head together, that's all. Had to learn to deal with uncertainty, to face it somehow. I can't really explain it, but whatever I was looking for in the woods, I guess I found."

"I'm glad," said his father, and his gaze was straight, his eyes clear, his smile genuine. "We're a tough lot, kid. We really are."

"How about you?" Dan asked. "How are *you* feeling?"

"Better than I was in June, that's certain. I'm going back to work in September. I've been on sick leave long enough."

"And the tests?"

"They didn't show much; but they did show that I've been making a nervous wreck of myself, that's what. The hand-shaking, the insomnia, the restlessness. . . . I've been in therapy for the last six weeks, getting some insight into what I've been doing to my body. I don't have to fear Huntington's disease right now as much as I have to fear myself. Strange, isn't it, how you can worry about the wrong things sometimes. It doesn't mean I'm home free. It doesn't mean the disease won't show up later. But right now we don't know whether I've got the gene or not, and I've wasted enough of my life worrying. It's one thing to know this with your head, though, and another to feel it in your gut and be able to do something constructive. But I'm getting there."

He accepted a platter of eggs that Blossom gave him and piled his own plate high.

"I guess I needed this time out too, Dan—to sort of get used to the idea. As an insurance actuary, I should have accepted the fact by now that I'm mortal; but it's something else to meet a fact face to face. Somehow I've got to make my peace with it."

"I know," Dan said. "I've been acting as though I'm entitled to a guarantee that I'll live a full life span; and nobody has that, not even kings and queens."

His father nodded. "It's not the only uncertainty we'll ever face. It's easy to think that if it wasn't for this, everything would be great. But that's not necessarily true."

Blossom sat down at her end of the table, listening to their conversation, and shoved the toast toward them, inched their milk just a little closer to their plates, kept an eye out on the butter and jam, and finally, when there was a pause, said:

"All you need is some fresh air away from those fumes in the city."

Dan's father smiled. "And country cooking. . . ."

"Absolutely."

"And eight hours of sleep a night."

"Positively."

"And a couple hours of chitchat a week with my mother."

"Of course!" Blossom laughed. "That's it exactly."

DAN WAITED until his father had gone back to Harrisburg and Bee had gone to the front bedroom for her nap. Then he quietly retraced his steps across the south pasture and headed for the woods.

It was important to find Oriole again, to know what had happened the day before. Had she found the coin in the water, perhaps, and given him Gabe's belt in exchange? Had he been there, his physical body on the bank, while another part of him returned to York? Had he fallen into some kind of trance, and the gypsies—frightened—moved on, taking the denarius with them?

Dan was not quite sure what path he had taken before, because it had been dusk when he'd entered the woods and dark among the trees. Now, in midafternoon, with the sun high overhead, nothing seemed exactly the same. There was no music to guide him, no smell of stew, no glimpse of color, no sound of laughter. Nothing but the August breeze and the occasional call of a bird overhead.

And then he sensed that he had taken the right path, was headed in the right direction. He remembered where he had stopped to estimate the location of the smoke. Yes, and here was where he had encountered Gabe. He hurried on, knowing his way now, turning the bend in the path where he had first caught the glow of their fire. Even if they had left last night, there would still be ashes, still be remains of a campsite.

He rounded the bend and then approached more slowly. There was the small clearing, the spot where the old green truck had stood, windows aglow in the twilight. There was the tree where the horse had been tethered, and the log where they had sat, eating their evening meal.

Where the truck had been before, however, there was a heavy tangle of vines. Where there had been bare ground, the weeds were knee-high. In place of the fire was a small dumping pit, filled with rusty cans, covered with a sloping canopy of spiders' webs. There was no point in even holding his hands over the ashes, for there were no ashes at all.

Dan did not ask himself how this could be, for there were no answers to any of the things that had happened to him lately. He had been here, he knew, and Oriole with him, and he clutched the belt with the eagle buckle.

Just as he turned to leave, however, as he stepped over the log, he saw there on top, carefully arranged, a patrin—the gypsy sign of direction. The sticks were placed in the shape of a cross, just so, with the longer one pointing the way they had gone. Dan looked in the direction of the patrin, and saw that it pointed toward the river. That was all he was to know.

He went back to the farmhouse, making a slow tour of the barn where Lonnie had sat, smoking his pipe in the hayloft. He wandered around the yard outside the house, but the footprints that had dried in the bare earth beside the window had somehow disappeared—dissolved perhaps, in a rain. He went inside and, with Blossom still sleeping, walked down the steps to the cellar where the spring bubbled up out of a crevice in the rock and the water ran out one wall into the sunlight.

"Ambrose?" he called softly. "Ambrose Faw?" and he waited.

But there was no reply. There were no shadows on the wall, no faces in the water, no sounds of distant singing.

What was the reality of it, then? The Faws had been there, and yet they had not. Was it possible that he, Dan, had not only experienced another age, centuries past, but that he and Blossom together, without their even knowing, had drifted in and out of another time, another summer—decades ago—and that the gray horse, like yesterday's fog or tomorrow's mist, appeared and disappeared at the mere whim of a magpie's call? The belt around his waist was real enough. It had been returned—when or how he wasn't sure. It didn't matter. The gypsies had gone, following the river, and—somewhere—were travelers still.

He wandered back up and sat on the glider till evening, the cat in his lap. He bantered with Bee as she moved in and out, and watched the fireflies rise up in the growing darkness beyond the screen. He milked the cow, fed the chickens, brought the horse inside the barn and shut the big doors.

Then he went upstairs to his room and walked slowly around it, examining everything as though seeing it for the first time, as though celebrating his return from a long journey: the patchwork quilt on the bed, the patterned wallpaper, the copper lamp hanging from the ceiling, the old tintype on the bureau of Suzanna Faa, and the painting of the storm at sea hanging over his bureau. He rested his arms on the bureau top and looked again at the captain's face.

And suddenly he noticed something he had not seen before—a pinpoint of red off in the distance. Strange, he thought, that in all the summers he had spent in this room, all the nights he had spent in that bed staring at the picture on the opposite wall, he had never noticed that small spot of color in the background. He took the picture down to see it better and saw that there was the outline of a ship, almost imperceptible, coming across the water toward the sinking vessel.

How was it that he had not seen it before? How was it he had mistaken the shadowy outline of the rescue ship for a dark cloud? The painting was not what it had seemed at all. What if the captain gave up at that very moment? What if the men in the water, holding onto a piece of timber, their faces exhausted from the ordeal, were to let go? What if the people in the lifeboat simply gave up in despair? No one saw the pinpoint of light in the distance, no one knew it was there. But did they have hope? Would they hold on?

He carefully hung the painting once more on the wall. What if he and his father just gave up? What if they allowed fear to overtake them when possibly, just around the corner, this year or next, there was a new discovery, a new medicine, new hope? What if Bill became so paralyzed at the thought of a nuclear war that he could not write editorials about it any longer or join any protest marches or volunteer his time in an organization for peace? What if he just turned the school paper over to somebody else who never worried, who didn't care? It was only a small paper, of course—less than two thousand students read it—but writing was the one thing Bill did best.

Dan thought of the gray sentry standing there on the wall of York, watching for the kings riding up from the south, or the messenger on horseback, or a ship returning home. A sentry for hope. That's what he wanted to be also.

He took up his notebook and pen, long unused, and sat down by the window overlooking the south pasture. It was not the people who went through life oblivious of danger who were the heroes. The real test of courage was whether or not you could face the truth.

Could you, knowing fully the horrors that might lie ahead, do what you could to stop them and then live for tomorrow, whether or not it ever came? Could you, after brooding and worrying and preparing for death, plan for living as well? Could you accept that there are odds in your favor as well as the odds against you, and that you might live a life as long and as full as any other? Would you be ready for that if it happened? These were the courageous ones —the people who lived with hope. He would put this in his article somehow. And when it was published, he would send a copy to Joe. He put his pen to the paper and began to write:

A GYPSY BURIAL

A Story of Life and Death and Hope on the Yorkshire Moors

by Dan Roberts

There was a letter from Joe Stanton the following day:

Dear Dan:
I feel, somehow, as I write these lines, that you know what I have to say before I put them down on paper. Nonetheless, I think you should know that the Roman denarius has found its way back to me.

How could it be, Dan wondered? It was only yesterday he had dropped the coin, yet the letter had been mailed four weeks before that. The present, indeed, was the past; the past itself, the future.

The story is a long one, but I'll not tell it to you in depth, for perhaps you know it already. I looked into the Ouse last week and saw, this time, a sentry. It has never happened this way before. Nor was my helmet Roman. I did not march across the moor, but walked instead along the wall at York.

It is a sad story of sickness and suffering and death, but I survived and so did a lad who came to me, bearing the silver denarius. When the episode had passed, I found myself not on the bank again, but standing far out in the water, drenched to the skin, conscious of the stares of strollers there on the bridge. When I got back to the bank and took off my shoes, I found, inside one of them, the Roman coin—the same, I feel sure—that Nat traded to you for your belt.

That same afternoon, I got in my cab and went to seek out the Faws, knowing how anxious Ambrose was to have the coin in their possession again. I found them this time in a town called Ripon. . . .

A town called Ripon. They had made it, then— Orlenda and Nat and Rachel. They lived.

. . . . and presented Ambrose with the coin without telling him the rest of the story. I felt suddenly, as I did so, that you would not want the money he had promised for its return. I

*don't know how I knew this, but the feeling was so strong
that I told him you sent it as a gift, with your regards, and
he sends his greatest thanks. This was most presumptuous of
me, I know, and if I was mistaken and you would have the
money, please post me a letter, and I will forward a cheque
to you at once.*

*There is news of the Faws, also. Both Ambrose and Rose
are well, though both have aged these last weeks, it seems to
me. Jasper is as he always was, but seems content enough to
play his fiddle and leave the running of the camp to others.
Rachel is now talking, a chattering little magpie, she is,
and the joy of her father's life.*

Orlenda has married. . . .

The words seemed to blur there on the paper,
the lines coming together, the ink fading. Dan had
to hold the letter tightly and force himself to read
on:

*Orlenda has married one of the Boswell clan, and he has
come to live in her camp in the tradition of travelers. He
seems a likable chap, a bit on the fun-loving side, perhaps,
but he has a good head on his shoulders and treats the
girl well. Ambrose is much pleased with the union, as it
assures him of someone to take over the* vardo *after he
is gone.*

Dan leaned back and closed his eyes. In every
corner of his room, the face of the dark-eyed girl rose
up before him, now laughing, now sad, now thought-

ful, now fast asleep, her head against his chest. He could sense her warm breath on his cheek, feel her soft hair on his arm, smell the scent of her skin. . . . He dropped his eyes to the letter again:

Nat has come to live with my wife and me. I never suspected how much he longed to break away, but when I came that day with the denarius, he asked if there was room for him at my house. With his parents' consent, he now makes his home with us, and we will send him to school in the fall. We have never had children of our own and are quite taken with having a young one about the place. It hurt Ambrose, I know, that the boy left, but Nat would never be happy as a traveler, and it was time, I suppose, that he followed the advice of his heart. At least Ambrose will see him often. Better than having the boy run off to a flat somewhere in London.

Do you remember the fortune that the old Granny once predicted for Ambrose and me? That a young buck would come into our lives and change it for either ill or good? We have decided, Ambrose and I, that the fortune has now come about. Only the young buck, of which it spoke, was different for each of us—the Boswell boy for Ambrose, and Nat, for the wife and me. All these years we thought it would be the same for both. It's strange, sometimes, how the mind grabs hold of a false idea and never wants to let go. We are getting old, I think. We need more thinkers in our time—people who will not go round and round over the same old ideas, but can see possibilities beyond other men's perceptions.

I do not think I will see the soldiers again, or the sentry either. Somehow, when I waded back to the bank that day, I thought to myself, "I've done with it, now." I've often puzzled how it was that I was a soldier at all. Had I been one once before in another time, I wonder? If I were young again, would I be one now? I don't know. To understand oneself, they say, one must know what his past has been. In any case, I have gone to the Ouse many times since to see if the soldiers were done with me. I have looked into the water and seen my own face, nothing more.

Perhaps it is over for you as well, and you can get on with your life. Forget if you will the night we clashed on the moor. But do think of me as your friend or, even better, as a footprint, leading you wherever it is you wish to go.

As always,
Joe

P.S. I am enclosing a note from Orlenda. It is as she sealed it, and I know nothing of what she writes. She pressed it in my hand the last time I was there and made me promise that I would post it to you.

Hesitantly, his fingers numb, Dan broke open the small envelope. The writing was more of a scrawl and full of misspellings, but he scarcely noticed:

Dear Dan:
It is surprise, I no, to hear from me, and I wonder if you even remember my name. I am thinking of you very much, and of the morning by the fire when you ask what my mother saw in your hand. I did not tell you then becase it is

not right, some say, for anyone to tell a fortune except the one who sees it. But it seem more wrong to me to cause someone to worrie, so I tell you what Mother sees. In your hand she saw a great fear coming upon you soon—that was all. Neither a good thing or a bad thing, only a fear. And so she tell you come back much later, becase she no that whatever it is that make the fear will be over by then. I am hoping that perhaps even now, the fear for you will be over. Maybe not. But whatever comes to you, my own wish is for good things only. I have ask my frind Joe Stanton to post this letter to you. Becase you are his frind, you are mine also.

Orlenda

The new hired man would be coming on Monday, and Blossom was readying the house. He was a clerk in the hardware store in Mt. Joy. In exchange for room and board, he had agreed to milk Blossom's cow and do her chores.

"Now don't go leaving your socks under the bed or anything," Bee chided as she bustled about the parlor. "I don't want to run the dust mop around up there after you've gone and find half a load of laundry."

"Hey, Bee, you sound as though you're glad to get rid of me," Dan said, setting his travel bag down by the front door. "You're going to miss me, whether you know it or not."

"I'll not miss you running off at night without telling me," she groused, determined to have the last word on it. Then she smiled broadly and came over to give him a hug. "Doesn't matter how old a woman gets, she misses her children when they're grown. It does me good to set two plates on the table at dinnertime. I get tired of talking to myself."

"What about the old tinker?" The words slipped out before Dan could stop them. He had promised himself that he would say nothing more, that he would not start something he could not finish, bring up a ghost he could not bury.

She studied him for a moment and her brows knit into a wisp of a frown over her nose. "You know, Dan, he's not been back. I've not seen his face in the stream for some time now."

"Are you glad?"

She thought about it. "Yes, I suppose so, now that a new hired man is coming. When an old woman gets so lonely she has to sit down and talk to ghosts, it's time they took her away, I imagine. Maybe the tinker didn't like what he saw. Maybe I talk too much. Whatever, he moved on and decided to let me be for a spell, and I'll not be leaving the cellar door open for him any more, I'm thinking; if death wants me now, he'll have to come get me. I won't make it easy."

They laughed, and there was a good feeling between them.

Dan checked his watch. "If Mother comes, tell her I went out to the south pasture to say goodbye to the horse. Be back shortly."

He set off across the field, going from patches of

sunlight to patches of shade as the wind blew the clouds over the sky. The horse moved away when he saw Dan coming, then thought better of it and let Dan come near, let him stroke the long nose, watching him with his huge brown eye.

Dan patted its flank and thought of Jasper, standing there by the cottage, grooming the horse that would carry Orlenda away. She was a Boswell now and would soon have children of her own. They would romp about her on the grass like cubs with their mother, and he wondered if, as she sat, she would sometimes think of an afternoon by the river, or a certain night on the moor.

He glanced over the fence toward the walnut grove and then to the woods beyond. There was no curl of smoke against the sky this time, no gray horse tethered to a tree, no faint sound of a fiddle.

He sucked in his breath, a swell of loneliness rising up in his throat, but as he turned to go, he saw something moving in the grass. He waited, and when it moved again, he walked softly over, a step at a time, to see what it was.

Instantly a young bird flew out, awkwardly flying to the top rail of the fence and then, in panic, to a tree beyond. A magpie. *One is for bad luck, two for good, three for a wedding, four for a death. . . .*

But the grass moved again, and Dan knelt down, searching with his hands. And there, cowering against the ground, its heart beating wildly, was a second bird, its feathers still downy, its tail not fully grown. It tried to get away, but tipped to one side, and Dan saw at once that its wing was broken.

He drew back, astonished, and then, longing to comfort it, took off his shirt and gently gathered the magpie up in it, stroking its head with one finger, holding it close.

The bird did not struggle. Once next to his chest, it lay still, as though entrusting itself to his care.

A magpie. How strange, it seemed, that it had been associated so often with misfortune. How peculiar that one small bird, so frightened itself of the world, should be seen as a portent of evil. A bird was all that it was—a fluff of feathers, a bill, a chirp, a heart that beat rapidly there in the palm of his hand.

Slowly he made his way back to the house, carrying the little bundle. *You've come a long way,* he said to the bird, *and there are still oceans ahead.*

SOMEWHERE SOUTH of Harrisburg, the Susquehanna changed color. Shadowy bluffs and deep water turned the river a darker green than it had been upstream. Rocky promontories jutted into the channel further down as it narrowed, the current flowing ever faster. At the end of the river, at its sand-lined mouth where whippoorwills called in the salt-tide marshes, a flock of magpies began their long voyage.

The black of their feathers, streaked with white, caught the sun as the birds charted their course by some primitive unknown in the depths below. They dipped or soared as the tide beneath them dropped or swelled, and neither the lure of the sky nor the threat of the wind could distract them.

On they flew, leaving the Susquehanna and traveling the length of the Chesapeake Bay—over the islands of Kent and Tilgman, of Smith and Tangier. The largest bird was in the lead, his eyes dark, his wings broad, with splashes of gray on his breast. It was he who followed the current, who gauged their time, who buffeted the winds with his body. For one moment, as they dipped low over the water, they were reflected not as black and white but orange and red, muted flashes of gypsy colors. Then the fog rolled in, a wind arose, and they headed out over the sea.